DOWN & OUT
THE MAGAZINE

vol 2, issue 1

EDITED BY
RICK OLLERMAN

Down & Out Books
3959 Van Dyke Road, Suite 265
Lutz, FL 33558
DownAndOutBooks.com

Cover photo © by Peter Rozovsky
Cover design by Lance Wright

ISBN: 1-64396-094-6
ISBN-13: 978-1-64396-094-4

CONTENTS

A Few Clues From the Editor
Rick Ollerman

You never write, you never call…

As you may have noticed, we've been on a bit of an unplanned and very much unwanted, somewhat spontaneous, hiatus. Although we've posted the news over the past few months, sent a few email notices, nothing makes up for the fact that we've just not managed to actually show up. I want to take a small amount of time to offer an explanation because truly, I think that all the wonderful readers and reviewers that we've managed to garner since we started this thing deserve more than a cavalier tip of the head and a wave.

A lot of us run into some kind of accident or event that can possibly disable us from time to time. Last July, being the cool cat cowabunga sort of dude I can't help myself from being, I was longboarding with my son. When I was his age, this plank with wheels would have been a mere "skateboard" but alas, no longer. At some point he stood with both feet on the front edge of the board. (This probably has its own name, too—a boat has its "bow"—but I've been suspecting I may not be quite up to the level of cool I once thought. In fact, I'm content in my ignorance in these finer points, much in the same way I'm perfectly happy not owning a pair of "skateboard shoes." Whether this may have contributed to subsequent events, I cannot be sure.)

So I wondered what would happen if I did the same thing. He must have had the good board because while he kept rolling on, my board shot forward and my body went backward. Like any good Neanderthal I thrust a wrist behind me, neatly fracturing the scaphoid bone in my left wrist.

I go on to learn that out of all two-hundred and six bones in the human body, this is the *only* one that has a single source of blood, just one vessel, that keeps it nourished. A common thing for expert longboarders who hang ten and land at just the wrong longitudinal and latitudinal coordinates in the Florida panhandle is to rupture this blood vessel, thereby killing the bone and requiring the wrist to be surgically fused.

Sounds severe, a permanent loss of flexibility and usage, but fortunately for me and quite in line with this long tale of good luck and fortune, mine was intact and I was only in for a long healing period—over a year. The doctor gave me a choice of having surgery to insert a pin to stabilize the joint, or to have it casted, in which case he assured me I'd be able to type and therefore work.

I'm no stranger to surgery. I've had a bunch. I'd have to think to come up with the precise number but it's something over a dozen. I'd like to say you'd be in for a treat if you saw my carefully shaped thighs or crafted buttocks but I've never had any cosmetic procedures done. My gut told me to have the surgery and get it over with; my general theory is that if you need to be repaired, it's best to get it done ASAP and get to the fun stuff, like physical therapy and opioid addiction. But no, I went with the cast.

This left me with a left hand that looked—and functioned—every bit as though I'd caught it in a woodchipper. I couldn't straighten my arm enough to be able to type with it and since doing what I do involves living on a keyboard, I'd effectively ended up hosing myself for four months. At first I thought the pain would subside and I'd be able to manage it but by the time it became clear it wouldn't, it was too late for the surgical option and I was stuck.

Like Annie from *Oklahoma*, I'd been afflicted with either an inability to say no, or else a vast over-estimation of my own ability to finish, um, anything, and I watched helplessly as I fell ever more and more behind.

Now I'll speed things up a bit. My kids go to school with a bunch of kids from countries all over the world. As a result, mere innocents like me can offer no defense against the sorts of global bugs, parasites, viruses and bacteria that appear to be our regular dinner guests. I came down with walking pneumonia (who names these things? For me it was clearly "bedridden pneumonia" or some such variant) which was a sort of half-living hell for another extended period.

And then, well, you know the joke about the new teen-aged driver and her dad's car? Yeah, me neither. In short, I found myself in two car wrecks in less than a thirty-six hour period of time, complete with a brain hemorrhage, concussion, broken nose, other broken bones, no car, and a little bit of sympathy for Enterprise, who found themselves also down a car. (My daughter, fortunately, was okay. She's a good seat belt-wearer.)

Doctors' orders had me off the computers and away from bright lights and brain activity for another extended period of time. At this point I've failed at a few deadlines, shed a few jobs, and have dipped beneath the surface five or six dozen times.

But wait, there's more...

My left shoulder was in want of repair and I went under the knife for that as soon as I was otherwise medically cleared. The surgeon fixed six separate issues that involve the rotator cuff, the biceps tendon, etc. I've had two surgeries on my other shoulder in the past and I can tell you that there's nothing like a shoulder for pain. It's like a full-grown alligator or great white is clamped on the joint with an unrelenting bite and it seems like there's no such thing as enough pain medication. In other words, ow.

So I'm at home, I'm in an immobilizing sling for six weeks, I'm doing physical therapy, and I'm supposed to be very careful about not letting my arm rotate exteriorly, or away from my body. Okay, sounds good, that's what the sling is for, and all that. It turns out, though, that the longer I sit or stand with the sling, it pulls down on the trapezius muscle on the top of my shoulder and causes its own set of problems, like pain and an inability to turn my head or tilt it up or down. I had to take the sling off for periods, which should have been fine, and I'd lay back on the bed, propped with ample pillows, one under my arm, wrist propped on my laptop keyboard.

But the best laid plans can be undone by the most adoring of wives and when mine came home from work one evening and gently laid her body tenderly atop mine, planting a tender kiss upon my love-starved lips, she then rolled off me to my left. Across my arm. Forcing it away from my body, exactly the way it was not supposed to move, and flattened it into the bed.

It hurt a lot. It still does. In fact, when I went back to the surgeon, he indicated I'm likely in for another surgery as soon as the rest of this one heals. In the meantime, I'm essentially a one-armed man with an eye out for Richard Kimble or Lieutenant Gerard.

And this is where I find myself now, actually in my replacement car on the way back from this year's Key West Mystery Fest, where a few years ago they asked me to become a "regular." In Key West? Well, okay. Sometimes you have to dig deep. This is as tight and intimate a conference as I've ever seen and it's a lot of fun with some good guests and very worth a Florida Keys vacation if you can manage it. On the other hand, outside of the conference activities, the bulk of my time was spent in the hotel room, working.

It wasn't enough, but it never is. Or at least it won't be for a while. But I'm trying. I've been saying the next thing I'm going to try is playing in open fields during lightning storms. What bad can happen?

There has been good news, too, and I would like to share it.

Last year we had two stories from this magazine nominated for Shamus Awards from the Private Eye Writers of America. We also had three or four stories included in Otto Penzler's near-mandatory annual *The Best American Mystery Stories* series entry, guest-edited by Louise Penny, in the Honorable Mention section. This is in addition to all the kind reviews in professional reviewers and publications like *Paperback Parade* and *The Digest Enthusiast*.

This year not only do we have two selections in a highly regarded anthology (and a third from *Blood Work*, a collection I put together that was published by the great people at Down & Out Books. Duane Swierczynski's story, "Lush," is one of the most fun crime stories I've ever read), Barry Lancet's feature story, "Three-Star Sushi," is up for two awards, the Derringer and a Shamus. I think the worst thing about having the unplanned break in production is possibly slowing down the worthy recognition we've been able to see blossom for a good number of the stories we've published.

I truly hope this issue simply continues from where we left off. The wonderful Walter Satterthwait is here with a brand-new story that, if we're all very fortunate, is only the first of a series. When I attempted to track Walter down to ask him about the possibility of wringing a new piece of writing out of him, I was happily surprised to find out he was living (at that moment) just a few miles away from where I was staying. Walter's in Greece for the summer, working on his first new novel in far too many years.

In the meantime, thank you for allowing me to share a little bit of my personal situation with you (while my new android body is awaiting my consciousness download) in a space I usually use to write about people I find much more interesting. The summer conference season is underway and if we all are in the same place, step up and say hello, just tap me on my good arm. This October, in Dallas, the Mystery Writers of America is putting on the 50th Anniversary version of the big one, Bouchercon, so if you've never been before, this'll be a party. Of course it'll be a bigger and better one with you there.

Down & Out is publishing the conference anthology this year, too, so that's the place to be if you want to pick up a copy and get it signed by as many contributors as possible. Regardless, there's no place better to meet authors and readers and hang out with a bunch of cool cats. But bring your own skateboards, I'm leaving mine at home.

Rick Ollerman

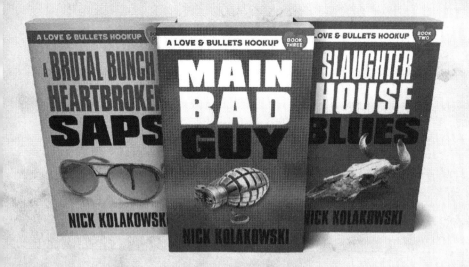

ACCLAIM FOR THE
LOVE & BULLETS HOOKUP TRILOGY
BY NICK KOLAKOWSKI

ShotgunHoney.com

*This is a great story to kick off this issue. I am by no means an expert on television history or even television shows (especially the popular ones). But April Kelly has to be some sort of pioneer in a ground-breaking and award-winning career that's spanned decades. For those of us in a certain age bracket, she's written, created and produced some of the touchstones of what was still at the time a very evolving medium. From the first ever TV show about a gay man, (*Love, Sidney*) and comedy classics like* Happy Days *and* Mork & Mindy *to musical specials and variety shows with John Denver, The Carpenters, and even The Starland Vocal Band (like you don't remember "Afternoon Delight"?), to shows like* Webster *and made-for-TV movies, she's been a force. Her work has literally spanned viewing generations: she created* Boy Meets World *and its later spin-off,* Girl Meets World. *Now I for one am willing to forgive her for all of this, even knowing that this is a far from complete tip of the iceberg sort of list. She tells me she even did some bad things under a pseudonym. You can check out an incomplete list of her credits on IMDB.com or better yet, just check out this tale about an ex-con just trying to make an honest living. Can you blame him for taking a shortcut or two?*

Rolling Gormay
April Kelly

I been cat-padding the taco meat for a year without anybody knowing or complaining, but then Mose, down to the pawn shop, started setting out poison to control the rats that seem to be the only thing reliably produced in this shit city since the steel factories got chink zip codes. The rats ate the poison, the cats ate the dying rats and, long story short, I might've killed four people.

The Rolling Gormay cruises Gary six days a week, providing delicious international cuisine—yeah, I know words like cuisine—to a customer base ranging from downtown hipsters swiping their smart-ass phones to homeless winos paying in damp, wrinkled dollar bills. The phones reek of snotty self-importance, while the Washingtons carry a whiff of body odor and lower-tier boxed wine. Diverse clientele is what I'm saying, which is why it took you guys so long to connect the dots.

I didn't start connecting them myself until the third one died, and when I heard his name yesterday on the 5:30 news, I only remembered it because he'd paid for his two tacos and diet Dr Pepper with a crisp C-note and had a conventioneer's name tag pinned to the breast pocket of the little boy suit grown-ass men have been duped into wearing by a fashion industry that obviously doesn't want them to get laid. You know the kind I'm talking about: waist pinched in, jacket and sleeves too tight and too short, makes a man look like a kid dressed for confirmation.

When the blond head filling the screen said it was strychnine caused the death and how it was mostly found in rat poison, I got a little niggle of recall. Hadn't Mose mentioned something about raining hellfire down on the rodents shitting up his counters every night and chewing holes in some Persian rug a cokehead frat boy hoped to redeem before his rich daddy noticed it missing from their townhouse?

Figuring I should do the responsible thing and check it out, I drove straight to the empty lot where I overnight the Rolling Gormay, not stopping in the backstreets where I'd been nabbing a couple free-range cats every nights. Way I see it, for the price of a tablespoon of cut-rate tuna, I get four or five pounds of usable meat and, like I said, no one ever caught on or complained. It allowed me to give good value for the price to my customers without running up my costs, and I made sure the cats didn't suffer. A snap of the neck and ten minutes later they were gutted, skinned and waiting in the cooler for the following morning's cook-up.

Backing the coach into the empty lot behind Mose Cander's Pawn Service & Estate Jewelry, I heard the usual crunch of beer bottles under my tires. I know it's technically a code violation to park and sleep where there's no sanitation link for my toilet and no electric, but Mose owns the property and it seems to me he ought to be able to say who gets to take advantage of it.

"Mose," I said, coming in the rear door shortly after he'd locked up the front. "You ever put out that rat poison you were talking about a couple weeks ago?"

"Bet your ass I did. Must have Dumpster'd fifty of the little sons of bitches in the last ten days. Why?"

"Just wondering," I said, which wasn't a lie. I was wondering how the hell *his* poison could of found its way into *my* taco filling.

"Rats weren't so damn thick around here in the old days," Mose went on to say. "Stray cats kept the numbers down. But, I don't know, there don't seem to be as many ferals as before."

That's when I started putting it together. The pussy population was down on account of me taking ten or fifteen off the streets every week. That had given the rats a free pass to party, causing Mose to set out the strychnine buffet. Cats eat rats; ipso facto, I'd cooked a few pre-laced with poison. Shit. Could it get any worse for a hard-working parolee just trying to make a living?

Sure it could.

"Hey, when Zeke Milton died last week, was it the cancer?"

"Well, when they found him, he was all twisted up and soaked in his own puke," Mose replied. "So I'm guessing more likely a mix of crank and sterno."

"Nobody checked?"

He looked at me like my fly hung open and a chipmunk was climbing out of it.

"Jesus, Frank, he was a homeless alky tweaker with a time bomb in his pancreas. Who would give a crap? Pick one from column A and put him in the ground."

"Only making conversation, hoss."

But I *did* give a crap how Zeke had died. He'd been my last customer that day. Poor twitchy bastard was a Vietnam vet, you know? Like my father. Mom always said that goddamn war made my old man the way he was. Anyway, Pop is decades gone but I have a soft spot for ex-mils who survived that governmental clusterfuck, so I always give them extra. My way of saying thank-you for your service. Zeke had asked for two tacos last week. It was the end of the day and there were a few scoops of filling left, so I overloaded the shells to give the dude a little extra protein. Next morning they found his body in the alley where he sometimes bedded down, but I had no reason to suspect a cause-effect situation. Of course, that was before I realized I was serving death on a corn tortilla.

After the news story aired yesterday about the dead convention-eer and before I headed to Mose's pawn shop, I checked online for any other strychnine deaths in Gary recently. I didn't recognize his name or remember the face, but another guy who had died same day as Zeke worked only a block from where I'd parked for twenty minutes during my normal lunch tour.

I still might of rode it out, you know? Pulled back on the meow mix and played it straight and dumb if law enforcement came around asking questions. But that option waved bye-bye around one o'clock yesterday while I was hustling to get to the final leg of my lunch route. I heard the *whoop-whoop* and checked the rearview mirror, then the speedometer. Blue lights in one and a speeding violation in the other. I pulled over and parked, taking out my license, mobile food permit and insurance card even before I heard both doors of the patrol car shut. By the time the two cops approached, I'd rolled down the window and plastered a smile on my face.

"Afternoon, Officers," I said, handing over my paperwork to the shorter of the two, a women around voting age. It was the older, taller male who spoke.

"You know the limit's thirty-five on this stretch of road, don't you, Mr.—?"

"Jessup," the lady cop helpfully supplied.

"Yes, sorry. I turned off Cameron a minute ago. It's forty-five there and I guess I forgot to ease off the pedal." I tried for a sheepish chuckle, hoping to get away with a warning.

"The sign's pretty clear, Mr. Jessup, but so many folks ignore it that my partner and I missed lunch while we were writing up tickets."

My mama didn't raise no fool, so I graciously extended an offer, careful to make it sound like a pleasure for me to help, rather than a bribe. The cost of two lunches would be a cheaper hit than a speeding fine, but I'd also be too late to get to the industrial park where I usually did a brisk trade. Manny Byrd would swoop in with his roach coach and co-opt all my regulars.

I went in the back, popped the awning and fired up the grill. She asked for a veggie burger on a wheat bun with light mayo, and he went with two Kosher hot dogs.

"Would you like coleslaw, beans or potato salad with those dogs?"

"I'll take all three."

Of course you will, I thought, keeping the smile pasted on while I turned to put a generous scoop of each on the sturdy paper plate before handing it over.

"So, how much do we owe you?"

A less observant person might've thought the request was genuine, but I had seen his eyes drop to the prison tat on my forearm, then lift to challenge me as I handed him his food. I was obviously not a guy who needed trouble.

"Please, Officer, it's on me," I said, careful to keep the sarcasm out of my voice.

He nodded and turned, taking only two steps before pausing.

"You know," he responded, facing the service window again. "Since there's no charge today, maybe I'll get a take-out order for my dinner tonight."

His partner had the decency to look embarrassed. She was okay with the simple math of free food equals no ticket, but not with a genuine shakedown.

He ordered four tacos and said he didn't want the shells to get soggy, so I wound up wrapping them in foil separately. After loading a lidded quart container with meat filling, I put shredded cheese, chopped tomatoes and iceberg lettuce in individual Ziplocs, then dropped a handful of hot sauce packets into the bag before passing it through the window.

I keep the seasoned cat meat in a five-quart slow-cooker, and the regular taco filling in my big, stainless stock pot. Every taco gets a heaping half-cup of meat, so I normally short-scoop from the stock pot, stir in a portion from the slow-cooker, then spoon the combo into a crunchy shell. Since Officer Hardass was being such a dick, I sent him on his merry way with a hundred percent Garfield. The seasonings are identical and I grind the cat to match the texture of my hamburger meat, so he'd never know the difference. And I'd get my sweet revenge for the extortion.

A few hours later I saw that newscast about the dead conventioneer, then went online and read about last week's strychnine death, finally visiting Mose and putting two and two together.

I didn't know his name or precinct. An anonymous phone tip would rain shit down on me whether it stopped that cop from eating the tacos or not. His partner would remember the name on the side of the coach and I'd be rotting in a Terre Haute cell before you could say "Chow-chow-chow." Time for Frank Jessup to disappear.

I was already parked outside my cousin Tyler's paint and body shop this morning at seven when he arrived to open up. I didn't give details, but I offered double if he could make my '98 Newmar Dutch Star look like every other motor home on the road by three. While Tyler worked his magic, I checked in with my parole officer to buy myself a couple weeks before he realized I'd ghosted, then boxed up the little bit of shit in my apartment worth keeping.

Tyler specializes in custom orders for extended family and vetted referrals, and he'd done a good job on the original paint for the Rolling Gormay, but I was genuinely impressed by his attention to detail on the makeover.

The finish didn't look guilty-fresh. He'd aged it a bit, even adding a couple fake rust spots below the driver's side window. One bumper sticker read "Proud Grandparents of An Honor Student," and the other "God, Guns & Country." In eight hours it had gone from a probable cause vehicle to a witness protection program on wheels.

I got the boxes loaded by five and was itching to hit the road, but I made one last phone call. Manny Byrd happily agreed to cover my breakfast and lunch routes while I flew to New Jersey to take care of my ailing mother.

Mom's buried right here in Gary and I was heading for Nevada, but I hoped the misdirect would smokescreen my getaway. I'd lay low for a while, repaint the coach with a new name, and open for business in Reno or Vegas.

And it would've worked, too, except before I even made it to the I-94 West on-ramp, some jackwad in a Humvee swerved to avoid hitting a dark shape that streaked across both lanes. When the Hummer sideswiped my rig I careened onto the shoulder, fighting the wheel to avoid going airborne. The coach overbalanced, tilted wildly, and went over on its side, skidding to a stop with a sickening screech of metal on gravel. Through the cracked windshield, I saw the ass end of a black cat sauntering away, his tail sticking straight up like a furry middle finger.

So, hand me that yellow pad and I'll write it all down, but seeing as I'm being cooperative as hell, how about you recommend I get a job in the kitchen.

Writing short stories and novels are two very different things requiring two very different skill sets. A short story isn't simply a matter of writing a small novel. There are a lot of very popular and successful novelists who turn the other way when they see me coming because they don't even want to think of me asking them for a short story (again). Of course there are many that will do both but it is a rare thing to find a writer who is actually good at writing in both forms. Enter the well-decorated and fellow New Hampsherite (when I'm not in Florida, anyway) Brendan DuBois. Brendan's one who not only didn't run away when I approached him for a story, he instantly and graciously told me yes. Yet for as warm and personable as Brendan is, he certainly brings a certain amount of properly chilled blood to this story.

The Good That Men Do
Brendan DuBois

It had been a long day but Cullen didn't mind. You took your days when you could, and rolled with everything that came your way. Embrace the suck when necessary. With his spotter Flint, he was on the fourth floor of a blasted-out office building, with a good view of the target area. They had spent all morning quietly setting up, finding the best observation point for the shot, two blocks down, to the entrance for one of the few operating luxury hotels left in this part of the city. What Cullen liked was that they were in an empty office with floor-to-ceiling broken windows that allowed them to hide deep inside, far away from any possibly curious eyes probing out there.

He was lying on a thin foam mattress, knee and elbow pads on, settled in, the stock of the M-24 Sniper Weapon System firm against his right shoulder, New York Yankees baseball cap on, bill reversed and down so it covered his neck, a stick of Wrigley's finest in his mouth. Clothing of blue jeans, black T-shirt, camo jacket. Fastened to a quick-release Bianchi holster at his waist was a 9mm Sig Sauer

P226 pistol. According to the time, the target should be arriving at the hotel in thirty-two minutes. Fine. He was ready. Question of the day facing Cullen was whether or not Flint was ready, for this was a two-part mission, to take out the target and to evaluate Flint for his role as spotter. This was Flint's first day with the unit and it was Cullen's decision as to whether he stayed or went.

So far the guy had been okay, but Jesus, he was one closed-mouth son-of-bitch. Cullen had respect for being quiet on a mission, but still, having a bit of to and fro helped pass the time, especially when they weren't providing overhead security for a patrol on the move, or protecting a Forward Operating Base somewhere, or doing long-range guard work for some visiting VIP. Today's job was a strictly wham-bam-round-to-the-head mission, so there was a lot of time to pass.

Cullen kept his breathing nice and regular, glanced at his Tag Heuer watch again, snug against his wrist and tactical shooting glove. Earlier Flint had smirked at seeing him wear the tactical gloves.

"Bare skin works just as well," he had said, adjusting a knob on his spotting scope.

And Cullen had said, "And gloves work just right for me, so let it be."

Now, it was thirty-one minutes. About five minutes away from when their target would arrive, he'd slide into the bubble, the zone, or whatever Zen bullshit you called it, when you blanked out all distractions and focused your entire group of senses on the mission. Cullen knew other snipers who would enter the bubble the minute they set up, all the way to those who just snapped-to about ten seconds out from when the trigger was pulled, but Cullen found five minutes out worked best for him.

Flint was about a half meter away from him, also stretched out, dressed identically save his ball cap was from Speer, one of the smallest yet best ammunition suppliers out there. In front of Flint on a small tripod was a Leupold Mark 4 12-40x60mm Tactical Spotting Scope. Cullen could see his target area quite clearly—it was a cool morning and the air was crisp and still—but Flint had a wider view of the hotel's entrance and surrounding sidewalks, and was in a good position to warn Cullen if something was coming into the target area, or if hotel security or members of the heavily outgunned and outmanned city police department were about to make an appearance.

Cullen said, "Everything okay over there, chief?"

"Just fine," Flint said. "Just fine."

Flint had a close-cropped black beard that was okay, but Cullen preferred the smooth-shaven look. Beards tend to stand out in crowds and people's memories, and Cullen liked to constantly depend on the forgetfulness of strangers. So that was one mark against Flint, though it wasn't a deal breaker.

Time check. Twenty-eight minutes.

Cullen said, "Remind me again where you're from?"

Flint grunted. "Here and there. Around."

Cullen said, "C'mon, sport, there must be more than that."

Through his telescopic sight and the sighting reticles, he saw two men hurry up the steps of the hotel, both well-dressed, both moving like they were nervous to be out in the open.

No answer from his spotter.

Oh well.

Cullen said, "I grew up in Millinocket, Maine. You ever hear of Millinocket?"

"Nope. Any reason I should have?"

"Yeah, you should. If you're a curious fellow."

"Then maybe I'm lacking in that department," Flint said.

"Maybe," Cullen said. "There are two reasons why you should know about Millinocket."

"What two reasons is that?"

The way through his telescopic site was still clear. Some traffic—pickup trucks, black Chevrolet Suburbans, a dented and rusted minivan—went past the hotel. Cullen said, "It was home to the Great Northern Paper Mill Company, one of the biggest paper mills in the country. Chances were, if you blew your nose or wiped your ass in-country, the paper came from Great Northern."

"Yeah," Flint quietly said. "Fascinating."

Cullen went on. "Damn right it's fascinating. One time it was the biggest paper mill in the country."

"Is it still the biggest?" Flint murmured.

"Nah, it got closed down a few years back, long after I got out."

"Really...the damn fascination quotient is really climbing. Okay, to the right, coming into your view. Two women. Jesus, look at the tits on the left. She's damn stacked."

Cullen watched the two well-dressed women come in and then depart his sight. Flint was right, the woman on the left was well-endowed, but still…He took a troubled breath. He said, "Reason I'm telling you this story is about my mom. I ever tell you about my mom?"

Another pause, and a loud sigh from Flint. "A mom story? Really? We're up in this damn shithole on an op and you want to talk about your mom?"

Time check. Twenty-four minutes.

"Hey, don't talk smack about my mom, all right? Thing is, she was a tough broad, and smart. Not school smart, but book smart. And street smart, too."

Flint said, "You mean they had streets out there in Millinocket?"

The thumping noise of an overhead helicopter temporarily blocked out their communication, and Cullen saw a brief shadow of the aircraft flicker over the hotel's entrance, like some dark angel's wings had suddenly blocked the sun.

"Lots of streets," Cullen said. "Lots of bars, too. There was me, my sister Kate, Mom and Dad. The two of them…they were like oil and water, you know? Fought all the time. Sometimes Dad won, sometimes Mom won, but one thing she never lost was being right in how she was gonna raise us."

Flint said, "Jesus, another looker, coming your way. Thought all the women in this part of the city were too scared to walk out by themselves during the day."

Cullen kept quiet, watched the young girl pass by, thick black hair, bright red lipstick, very tight and short black skirt, and then went on. "Mom always said to my Dad, Henry—that was his name—Henry, you may have helped bring these kids into the world, but I'm gonna raise 'em the way I see fit. And if you want to live to our golden years together with your balls still attached, you goddamn better let me."

Another sigh from Flint. Cullen hated to admit, but his spotter was starting to get on his nerves. "A hard-ass, then?" Flint finally asked.

"Oh, man, I'll tell you how hard-ass. The Marines…by the time I went to Camp LeJeune, I went through basic and thought, shit, this was nothing. Nothing! Should have grown up in Millinocket, when in winter you had to shovel out the sidewalk and the driveway, and the driveway of Mister Morneau, our disabled vet neighbor. In the summer, when you had to mow the lawn, keep the place tidied up, do chores all the time, no A/C at night…and by the time you could walk down the block by yourself, you got a job. Picking up trash, mowing lawns, finding aluminum cans for the recycle center, Mom did a lot of things, but she made me ready for the Marines, that's for damn sure."

"Gee," Flint said.

Cullen went on. "But that wasn't the most of it. There was a small Catholic school nearby and Mom insisted me and Kate go to it. Even though it meant a long bus trip, and paying tuition that we couldn't afford. Hell, we didn't go to church that much, but Mom said the schools would give us a good education, plus teach us about being good."

Flint said, "Hunh? What do you mean, being good?"

"Yeah. Good. Good versus evil, you know. Real basic religious shit. I wasn't sure what she meant at the time, but I heard her yelling to Dad once, about him and his brothers and his whole damn family."

Gunshots broke out two or three blocks away. Cullen didn't bother to move; the familiar noise didn't even make him blink.

Time check. Nineteen minutes. Cullen said, "She told Dad that he and his brothers and uncles, and all that, they were brawlers, they were hell raisers, and most of 'em ended up in jail at one time or another. County, state, hell, even Federal—one of my uncles did some serious time in Leavenworth. My mom said, I'm gonna teach my kids the difference 'tween good and evil, and make sure they get their heads squared on right, and leave town with their heads held high."

Flint said, "Your sister good looking?"

Cullen nearly lifted his head from the rifle stock. "What the hell does that have to do with anything?"

Flint said, "Relax, I was just asking. Sounds like a tough place to grow up, tough place to live. If your sister was good looking, I could see your mom having problems keeping her…well, you know, keeping her out of trouble."

Cullen let out a breath. "Yeah, that was the case, all right. Kate was a looker but she was smart, she had my mom's brains. She let the boys touch and play with her, but never go all the way. She always said she wasn't going to end up knocked-up in some trailer park outside of town, with only a high school education. She's a bank exec now back in Manhattan. It was me that Mom had trouble with…"

"She have trouble with all your yapping?" Flint asked. "Hold it…taxi cab slowing down from the right…"

The dented and scraped yellow Crown Vic slowed down, just as Flint said, and then it sped up. Cullen said, "No, not my talking, not at all. But between my mom during the night, and the nuns during the day, they really pounded into me the difference between right and wrong, good and bad. You see, Mom thought the way I was brought up, with my dad's family, I was…whaddya call it, predisposed to do evil things, to be a criminal. Mom thought she was gonna prevent that with all this schooling and shit. She said I might have the urges, the temptations, to do bad, but she and the nuns were gonna brake that."

"Break it, like smashing a dish?"

"No," Cullen said. "Brake it like a car brake or truck brake."

"Oh," Flint said. "You think all that messing around with your mind took?"

A good question, one that actually caused a few sleepless hours there and there. Cullen went on. "Some days, I like to think so, boss. Heck, about three weeks ago, I was at a supermarket, went into one of those self-checkout lines, the ones where you scan your own groceries."

Flint grunted.

"I went through, had a container of tomatoes, couldn't get the damn thing to scan. The label was scraped. Tried three times. No joy. I looked around. Nobody from the supermarket was nearby, they were all hanging around at the other end of the regular cash registers. It would have been so easy to toss those tomatoes into my shopping bag, walk out. Who would know? Thing was, I would know. That's what Mom taught me. That I would know that I had done bad."

Another grunt from his spotter.

Time check. Twelve minutes. Through the scope and reticle, his muscle memory started coming back, from his scores of previous kills, with that sweet anticipation that out there somewhere was a man—living, breathing, thinking—who had a meet-up in less with twelve minutes with Cullen, his rifle, and a copper-jacketed 7.62 mm round. No matter what that man dreamed, plotted and prayed, his destiny would be coming to a bloody end in mere minutes.

Cullen said, "I mean, look at this city, this country, the way this whole place is all screwed up. Why did that happen?"

Flint kept quiet. Cullen wasn't dissuaded. He said, "People forget the basics. About right and wrong, good and evil. The basics, you know? And when they forgot about the basics, about what made civilizations work, they went back to tribes, clans, families...no longer worrying about the whole picture. So what happens then? Things fall apart. Water stops running. Power flickers and goes out. And you and me and others are sent out to clean things up."

Again, Flint was quiet. His spotter didn't know it but he was now on the slippery slope that was going to end with his termination. Cullen said, "All of us have that capability of evil. It's up to... whatever you want to call civilization that makes the difference."

"Unh-hunh." Flint said, "Time?"

Cullen checked his watch. "Seven minutes."

Just two more to go.

"Flint?"

"Yeah?"

"You understand what I'm saying?"

"No offense...but not really."

"Fair enough," Cullen said. "You got anything on your mind, at all?"

"Nope. Just getting the job done."

Cullen checked his watch. Five minutes.

"Okay, let's get the job done."

He regulated his breathing, eased into the time, the space, the bubble, the Zen. Whatever. Another gunshot echoed out there. A long-away drone of a siren. Another flash of shadows as a helicopter flew overhead.

Breathe, focus.

Breathe, focus.

Breathe, focus.

Flint's voice: "Motorcade approaching from right."

Breathe, focus.

Breathe, focus.

In the zone.

All hail the zone.

"Motorcade should be visible."

The zone.

"Motorcade's come to a stop."

19

Zone.

"Yours."

Black Cadillac Escalade, with tinted windows, snapped into view. Waiting.

Doors opened up, a scrum of bodies milling around. In the rear, the four steps leading up to the entrance of the hotel.

The bodies moved as one to the stairs.

Now.

Target in clear view. Cullen had studied the target's face and body for weeks so when the target had its back to him, Cullen knew he was his.

In the past he'd always gone for body shots, for then it wasn't a damn shooting competition, but an urban battleground where a shot to the chest or the gut got the job done quick. But this one was going to be different. If this high value target was wearing body armor underneath that fine Savile Row suit, Cullen had to make sure the mission got done. He only had time for one shot.

His finger moved.

Gunshot.

Stock punched against his shoulder.

Flint said, "Got it."

Cullen started moving, not saying anything, getting the gear together, wanting to get the hell out.

Flint joined him.

Fourteen minutes later they were in another part of the city, among blocks and blocks of abandoned or destroyed homes. In the rear of the small house was a white GMC rental sedan and they had quickly changed into fancier civilian clothes, with Cullen leaving the gloves for last. They were in a kitchen area, covered with dust, mold and animal droppings, their gear dumped on a wooden table in the center. The stove had been pulled out and the small refrigerator had been overturned on the floor.

Flint said, "Good shot."

"Thanks."

"Bet everyone in that group is probably changing their underwear."

"Probably," Cullen said, now in casual slacks, polo shirt, still wearing his shooting gloves and Yankee baseball cap. "Look, we need to debrief."

Flint glanced at his watch. "We got the time?"

"Plenty of time."

In the distance was another gunshot, and then another siren.

Cullen said, "Not going to sugarcoat it, Flint. You don't communicate well. You don't respond well to me, the shooter and team leader, and in addition, you've got a rotten attitude toward women."

"Say freakin' what?" Flint asked, eyes hard.

"You heard me," Cullen said. "Talking about hot looking women. Checking out their tits. Neither respectful or professional."

Flint's voice was strained. "You do what you need to pass the time."

"Maybe," Cullen said, looking over the gear on the table. "Thing is, you haven't been trained well. You don't take care. You don't pay attention."

"The hell...we made the shot, we got out. What else do you want?"

"Remember when I was talking about my hometown, about Millinocket? I said there were two reasons you should know about Millinocket. One was about the paper mill. But you never asked me about the second did you?"

Silence from Flint.

Cullen said, "Remember? Two reasons? And you never asked me about the second reason."

In a strained voice, Flint said, "All right. What's the second reason I...or anybody else...should care about Millinocket?"

Cullen forced a smile. "Long time ago there were a series of Maine humor sketches, created by a guy named Marshall Dodge. Called *Bert and I*. One of the most famous pieces is about this out-of-towner, asking a Maine old-timer how to get to Millinocket. The old-timer goes through a variety of directions, and finally gives up. He says, 'Come to think of it, you can't get they-ah from hey-ah.'"

"So?"

Cullen sighed. "You should have asked. You should have shown curiosity. You should have shown initiative. Sorry, that's a game-stopper."

Flint stood there, quiet, eyes glaring. Flint said to Cullen, "Why are you still wearing gloves?"

Cullen said, "I think you know why."

He flipped out his Sig Sauer and shot Flint in the right eye.

* * *

Thirty-two minutes later, Cullen was in the North Terminal at Detroit's Metro Airport, ready to catch his American Airlines flight to Miami after having dropped off his rental car and unnecessarily tipping the young Hispanic man who took the keys from him. Just before he got to the gate he walked past a large Somali family, clad in their traditional Muslim clothing, and in trying to pass over a water bottle to a young boy, the mother dropped the bottle and it rolled out onto the concourse. Cullen scooped up the bottle, passed it over to the smiling mother.

In Arabic she said, "*Shokran Gidan*" and he replied, "*Afwan*," and kept on walking. He then stopped at a Champps Restaurant & Bar and had an iced tea and chicken Caesar salad. Nearby were a group of six soldiers who were sitting in a group in their BDUs, loudly having lunch. When Cullen left, he slipped two hundred-dollar bills to their waitress to cover their bill.

Now he was at his gate, with an hour left before his flight was going to be called. He took out a burner cellphone, dialed a phone number in Maine from memory, and the old but still strong woman answered.

"Hey, Mom, it's your favorite son," he said, knowing he was surprising her, happy at the feeling.

"Hah," she said. "Favorite son indeed."

"Ah, Mom, come on, don't start."

She laughed. "You still being good?"

Cullen looked up at one of the hanging television sets displaying CNN, which was reporting on a Detroit shooting. Not one of the passengers or airport workers walking by gave it a glance.

"You know it, Mom," he said.

This is a nice project to bring to these pages. Ray Daniel is another short story writer, a Derringer winner at that, with a story mentioned in the 2013 volume of Otto Penzler's The Best American Mystery Stories *(see more about that in the introduction to this issue), as well as a novelist with his series about a tech savvy Boston-based widower named Tucker. Kellye Garrett describes herself as a "recovering Hollywood writer" who exploded onto the crime fiction scene with her debut novel,* Hollywood Homicide *in 2017. The book was nominated for award after award, winning many of them, which only continued with the other books in the series. In this entry, Ray and Kellye combine to give us a taste of both of their writing worlds, bringing Ray's Tucker together with Kellye's Dayna in an east coast meets west coast story of street justice.*

Code Switch
Ray Daniel & Kellye Garrett

She brought the man to the little room she shared with another on Front Street. The rum on his breath was strong and when she began to do what she always did for them, what they liked and paid her for, this one pushed her away. His hand was on her neck as he turned her. She tried to fight him but his grip was tight and the way he squeezed weakened her. Once her resistance was gone, he took what she swore she would never give any man. Later, when she was able to get out of bed she saw the money on her night table. He had paid double what she usually charged for services. Of course he wanted to do right by her.

If aliens invaded Los Angeles, Tucker was certain they would gather on the tarmac of LAX and worship the saucer-like building that dominated the airport. He stood in disorienting February warmth and raised his phone, snapped a picture of the building and tweeted.

@TuckerInBoston: I, for one, welcome our alien overlords. #vacation

February in Boston had been depressing. The city had been hit by three snowstorms in two weeks, forcing Tucker to sit in his condo watching Montreal snow removal videos as if they were porn: *That's it, baby, fill those dump trucks, now dump it in the river. Oh yeah!*

With another storm on the way, Tucker had decided it was time to visit California. His plane had taken off just as the storm's first flakes were drifting down onto Logan. Now, standing in LA's sun, Tucker summoned a Lyft ride. The app told him that he'd be picked up by the phonetically correct *Dayna,* in an Infiniti.

Dayna texted: Be right there.

A Pepto-Bismol colored Infiniti appeared, scooting in front of a black Range Rover idling at the curb. Tucker opened the front door.

"Dayna?"

A pretty and oddly familiar black woman beamed back at him. "Aloysius?"

"You can call me Tucker."

"You don't go by Aloysius?"

"Would you?"

"Good point. Hop in."

Tucker tossed his bag in the back seat and sat in the front next to Dayna.

She asked, "You ever considered going by Al?"

"You ever considered dropping the 'Y'?"

"The Y's for my grandmother. My mother would kill me, and then she would kill you."

"Better keep the 'Y,'" Tucker said, looking forward. Instead of moving, the car sat at the curb. "Are we waiting for something?"

"Someone." She glanced at the cell phone mounted above the radio. "Someone named Dagger." She leaned toward him and whispered, "You did Lyft Line."

"And that means…"

"It means you're sharing a ride."

"With someone named Dagger."

"Yep."

The back door opened and a guy dropped into the seat, throwing a tiny man-purse on top of Tucker's bag. The guy wore white pants, a cowl-neck sweater, and a brown suede jacket sporting so much fleece that Tucker was sure it had a name and would one day befriend a lonely child.

"Drive," the guy said.

"Dagger?" Dayna asked.

"Drive!" he said again. "Drive drive drive!"

"Where?"

"It's in the app."

Dayna put the car in gear.

As Dayna pulled out Tucker looked past Dagger and his pet jacket to notice three guys, a big one, a little one, and one in a sports jacket, jump out of their black SUV, swear (an easy lip read), jump back into the car, and pull out. Unusual behavior for back home in Boston, but maybe typical in LA.

Dayna asked, "So, Tucker, where you from?"

"Boston," Tucker said.

"Boston?" Dagger said. "You're from Boston?"

"Yup."

"Shit! Shit! Shit!"

"Dagger," Tucker asked, "are those guys in the SUV from Boston?"

"What SUV?"

"The one behind us."

Dagger looked out the back window. The guy riding shotgun gave him the finger.

"Shit!"

"What's going on?" Dayna asked.

"Looks like Dagger's got his own version of Lyft Line. He's bringing friends," Tucker said.

"Fudge," Dayna said.

Cover your bills, the Lyft website said. *Make money. Be your own boss.* It didn't say anything about being followed by three guys from Boston.

The only thing that kept Dayna from stopping the car and throwing Tucker and Dagger out was her perfect Lyft rating—and denial.

"No one's following us," she said but glanced back anyway. The airport exit neared. She didn't take it, instead opting to drive to the next terminal. The SUV followed. They were definitely tailing them. "Why would someone want to know where we're going?"

"Ask him." Dagger pointed at Tucker.

"Me?" Tucker said. "I just got here."

As the two argued, Dayna decided to use LA traffic to her advantage. At Sepulveda she entered the lane for the 105 onramp, the SUV on her bumper. Then she waited. When she saw her opening, she hit the gas, yanked the wheel, and pulled the Infiniti back on the main stretch of road. Tucker and Dagger stopped bickering as the car careened into the left lane and made an LA left-on-red onto Imperial Highway. She checked the rearview in time to see SUV attempt the move, only to be met by a wall of LA drivers who took lane changes as a personal affront.

Once she was sure they were safe, she spoke. "Did we decide why we're being followed yet?"

"Because of my boss," Dagger said. "Eddy Washington."

"Wow," Dayna said.

"Who?" Tucker said.

"You've never heard of Eddy Washington?" Dayna asked. "Highest paid black actor on television. Runs the E.W. Foundation for Racial Injustice?"

"Sorry," Tucker said.

Dayna and Dagger shared a look: *Straight white guys.*

"Dagger, what's going on?"

Dagger waved his phone. "It's about a video."

Dayna checked the mirror. The SUV was gone so she pulled into a parking lot to watch cell phone footage shot by someone in a car with Eddy. Eddy sat in the driver's seat. His skin and hair were both the lightest of browns. His piercing gray eyes broke up the monotony. He wore a Red Sox cap. The video seemed familiar although Dayna couldn't place why.

She watched as a cop showed up and put his head through Eddy's open window.

"Long way from Roxbury, aren't we?"

The screen went black.

"Wow," was all Dayna could say.

"What am I missing here?" Tucker asked.

"A few years ago Eddy got arrested by a racist cop near Boston. Someone leaked the dashcam video. It went viral. Eddy became famous overnight for DWB."

"DW what?" Tucker said.

"Driving While Black," Dagger said.

Dayna said, "Everyone wanted the cop fired, especially Eddy. And the cop actually lost his job—for once. This is from that night, but it isn't the dashcam video. Dagger, who sent this?"

"I'm guessing someone in that SUV," Tucker said.

Dagger said, "Someone anonymously emailed it to me saying to show it to Eddy because they wanted to meet."

"What did Eddy say when you showed it to him?" Dayna asked.

Dagger's look said it all—he hadn't.

"You skipped town?"

"Yes, and I blocked their email account."

Dayna rolled her eyes. At least this mess wasn't hers. "I'll drop you both off wherever you want."

"Works for me," Tucker said. "I have tickets for Universal."

"Well, this is not good." Dagger shoved his phone back in Tucker's hands, the Twitter app open to the direct message screen: *"We're going to kill you and your friends."*

Attached was a photo of Dayna and Tucker sitting in the car.

"Idiots," Tucker said. "Nobody ever dies from an internet death threat."

"There's always a first time," Dayna said.

Tucker sat in the Farmer's Market sun eating a classic green apple pie from DuPar's with a delicious side of schadenfreude. He scrolled through his Twitter feed following the hashtag #snowhell where Boston citizens shared stories of a city buried by a Nor'easter.

Tucker wasn't going to let this threat thing bother him. Instead he enjoyed his pie and read Twitter as Bostonians whined about the snow.

@bosdriver: Literally living through the worst weather in the world #snowhell #BostonStrong

Tucker took a picture of his pie and the sunny market and tweeted it.

@tuckerinboston: I got the #snowhell out of there! #pietime

He glanced up. Dayna stared at him, Dagger peeking over her shoulder.

"You're too obvious out here," she said.

He took a bite of pie. "Can't waste a beautiful day like this."

"They're *all* like this!"

"Doesn't mean we should waste it."

"Dagger told those guys to meet us here."

"And that's how I'm going to dox them, but I need a picture."

"You can eat that in the upstairs patio," Dayna said. "We'll see them from there."

"But I like it here."

"You might not take a death threat seriously, but I do. I'm not getting killed for someone who hasn't even tipped me yet."

Dayna harrumphed off with Dagger in tow. After a moment Tucker followed, making sure to take his pie.

The three sat in the upstairs patio and watched.

"They're here." Dayna said. Tucker recognized the big guy, the little guy, and the guy in the blazer from the SUV. They stood outside Phil's Deli and Grill looking around and arguing.

Tucker said, "We can't see their faces from up here. If I were still at my table, I could get a shot."

"And probably get shot," Dayna said. "Death threat, remember? How do we make them look up?"

"We don't." Tucker rose and headed for the staircase.

"You can't go down there," Dayna said.

"Yeah? Watch my pie."

Downstairs, Tucker approached the three guys still in front of the deli and raised his phone. The three recognized him just as he took the photo.

Tucker put the phone in his pocket. "You guys try the pie?"

"The what?" the big one asked.

"The pie. It's very good. Home made."

"You took our picture?" asked the little one with red hair and freckles.

Tucker stood ten feet away. "Yup."

"Delete it, you asshole!" said the third guy in the blazer. The brains of the operation. Maybe.

"Too late," said Tucker. "Already in the cloud."

"You're the guy with Eddy," Blazer said.

"No. I'm the guy on vacation. But I can get a message to Eddy."

The big guy said, "Let's take him."

Tucker waved around at the Farmer's Market bustle. Mothers feeding kids ice cream. A big guy devouring a pastrami sandwich. "Public place."

Blazer said, "Tell Eddy he's a long way from *Roxbury*." He made air quotes around Roxbury.

Blazer turned and left. The other two followed.

The early 21st century would, one day, be heralded as an era of anonymity, a golden time when the only people who could be recognized on the street were celebrities. Then facial recognition technology came along and that time was over.

Dayna, Dagger, and Tucker sat in her Infiniti as Tucker ran a doxing app on his phone.

Dayna said, "This whole thingamajig you got going on sounds farfetched."

"Trust me, I got this."

"What does this app do?"

"It compares someone's photo to all social media profile pictures."

"They can do that?" Dagger asked.

"Worse," Tucker said. "Anyone can do that."

The app beeped.

"Their names are Nickels Murphy, Ticky O'Sullivan, and Bob."

"Bob?"

"Yeah, his Facebook profile just says Bob. He's the guy in the blazer. Nickels is the big one. Ticky is the little one. All three are from Charlestown."

"Charlestown?"

"Next to Boston," Dayna said. "Didn't you see *The Town*?"

"I thought that place was fictional."

"Also, they have entries on mugshots.com."

"Even *Bob?*" Dayna looked at the display.

"Robert P. McGillicutty."

"I see why he goes by Bob," she said.

"What'd they do?" Dagger asked.

"Bet they robbed a bank," Dayna said. "Charlestown."

"Nice. Just 'cause they're from Charlestown," Tucker said.

Tucker read on and winced.

"What's it say?" Dayna asked.

"They robbed a bank."

"But what does that have to do with Eddy?" Dagger asked.

"Let's ask Eddy," Tucker said. "Any idea where he'd be?"

Dayna said to Dagger, "The Global Healing Ball, right?"
Dagger nodded. "You'll never get in."
"Challenge accepted."

Dayna stood a block away from the ball as the Lyft Luxe Mercedes
pulled up. She was wearing black Alexander McQueen. If the dress
were two inches higher and the party were two miles east, someone
would have mistaken her for a hooker. She opened the rear passenger
door to find Tucker in a beige Polo, faded Levi's and, as if it
couldn't get any worse, white Skechers. "Thought we agreed to
dress up."

"We did," he said. "What's wrong?"

Fashion disaster.

"It's fine," Dayna said and they drove off.

Their driver joined a conga line of cars dropping off guests.

"Whatever you do, don't make eye contact, don't stop moving,
and don't speak," she said. "No matter what happens, just go with
it. Okay?"

"Got it," Tucker said.

At the front of the valet line, the driver made a big deal of opening Dayna's door. Dayna got out first and surveyed the scene. A
producer with too much money, yet not enough Oscars, had offered
to host the Global Healing Ball at his 15,000 square-foot Beverly
Hills bachelor pad. A stick-figure blonde checked in guests. Two
juiced-up security guards ushered them into the backyard entrance.

Tucker stepped out of the car.

"Wow."

She threw him a look.

He ignored her. "There's no way we're getting in there."

"Trust me, I got this."

"Touché."

She was too busy watching the group get out of the car behind
them to respond. An entourage followed Kandy Wrapper, singer of
the number one song in the country. The group moved to the front
of the line. Dayna let them pass, then sidled next to them. Tucker
followed.

"Love your dress. Givenchy?" Dayna asked the woman bringing
up the rear.

The woman smiled. "Couture. Saw it at their runway show last month and had to have it."

And they were off, chatting about haute couture. Soon they breezed past the hulks and right into the party. Until the security guards made Tucker.

"Polo?" one asked.

Dayna put her arm through Tucker's. "Honey, I told you no one would get the irony."

"Oh," one security guard said. "That's funny!"

"Friggin' hipsters," said the other.

Dayna smiled. "I can't take him anywhere."

Tucker nodded and shrugged and she pulled him inside.

"Nifty social engineering," Tucker said.

"Told you to trust me," Dayna said. "Now, let's find Dagger and Eddy."

They found them in a spare guest house. When Tucker and Dayna stepped inside, everyone turned, looked them over, and returned to their conversations.

"What was that?" Tucker asked.

"LA's version of hello. We might have made some new friends, but you're wearing Polo."

Dagger waved them over to Eddy who ignored Tucker, focusing his attention on Dayna.

"Queen, you are beautiful. It's a pleasure to meet you."

"Thanks," Dayna said then jumped right into it. "Did Dagger explain the situation?"

"Only that some fans wanted to meet."

"It's a little more than that," Tucker said. "Have you seen the video?"

Eddy shook his head. "Don't need to. Dagger will take care of it." He focused back on Dayna. "Why don't you act anymore?"

"I retired. Why aren't you taking this seriously?"

"Because haters come with the job, especially when you're successful and black in America. I remember those commercials you were in. You were amazing, even though they had you hawking fried chicken."

Dayna couldn't disagree, but that wasn't the point. "You should look at the video."

Eddy shrugged her off. "We could get you a guest spot on my

show. I'm all for helping my fellow black actors, especially ones as talented as you. What do you think?"

She thought someone doth compliment too much.

Eddy was clearly trying to avoid talking about the video. He continued his pitch. "You could play my ex-girlfriend. College sweetheart—"

"Bob says you've come a long way from *Roxbury*," Tucker said.

Eddy turned to him, his voice a little too calm. "Who is Bob?"

Tucker shrugged.

Eddy said to Dayna, "Dagger and I got somewhere to be. You be good, Queen."

And with that Eddy left. Dagger threw them an apologetic look over his shoulder.

"He's hiding something," Dayna said.

"Or Bob the felon is lying. I'd go with the second one."

"Someone's lying." She just wasn't sure who. "And I'm starving."

Tucker said, "Let's forage."

Dayna and Tucker were on their fourth chicken skewer when they heard the scream from the tennis court.

"Eddy!" Tucker said, but Dayna was already heading toward the sound. Tucker followed.

We should have never let him leave." Dayna kicked herself. Eddy hadn't made the best first impression but she didn't want the guy hurt. "Please let him be okay."

The crowd blocked her path. She knew Eddy had to be somewhere in the middle of it. She and Tucker pushed through, Dayna repeating, "Please let him be okay."

They squeezed to the front.

Dagger lay on the ground, a knife in his chest.

"Nobody ever died from an internet death threat, huh?" Dayna said.

"Shit," Tucker said. "There's always a first time."

Tucker sat in his hotel room, wide awake at the ungodly hour of six in the morning, remembering the unfathomable meanness of LA police officers.

"Hey, Ralph Lauren, you're next," the lady cop had said.

"Who me?"

"Who else is wearing a Polo shirt?"

Great—a mean-girl cop.

"That's just unkind."

"So's stabbing a guy in the chest."

"But—"

"I don't see your name on this guest list...Aloysius."

"Please call me Tucker."

"Your name still isn't on the list."

"I heard there'd be chicken skewers."

"And you just walked in?"

Tucker shrugged.

"So much for security," the cop said. "Okay, you can go."

Tucker muttered. "Beat LA."

"What?"

"Nothing."

Tucker had gotten to his hotel and fallen into bed. Jet lag woke him four hours later. Now he sat with a pot of coffee, a muffin, and a stunning view of the Los Angeles lights winking out as the sun rose. His phone rang.

"You up?" Dayna asked.

"It's ten in the morning back home. I've been up for hours."

"Eddy needs us."

A few minutes later, the Pepto-Bismol Infiniti pulled up in front of the lobby and Tucker got in.

"I thought Eddy had chalked this up to a fan," Tucker said as they pulled onto Sunset Boulevard.

"He changed his mind," Dayna said. "Murder tends to do that to people."

"What's he need us for?"

"Eddy doesn't want any emails flying around."

"So he sent you to get me."

"Least I can do."

The car drove past Mel's Diner, reminding Tucker that it was mid-morning in Boston. Maybe time to get another cup of coffee. Before he could say anything they were driving through Sunset Plaza.

"Weirdest thing," Tucker said. "Why would three guys from Charlestown pick on Eddy?"

Dayna shrugged. "Why would a cop pull someone over when he wasn't breaking any laws?"

"Yeah, but why would they—"

"I mean, they *are* from Boston."

A knot tightened in Tucker's gut. "What's that supposed to mean?"

"It has a reputation. Even I've heard about how racist it is, and I'm from the South."

"That's just bullshit."

"And how would you know?"

"I live there."

"Your friends think so, too?"

"They love it as much as I do."

"Really? Your black friends?"

Tucker crossed his arms, watched palm trees glide by.

"You don't have a black friend, do you?"

"Of course I do. Back when I had a job we had a black engineer on the team. At school we had three black kids in class from Metco."

"You have to go back to elementary school to find a black person you know? And you still talk to these childhood besties?"

"Yes."

"Liking their Facebook statuses doesn't count."

"I made one friend at MIT. One."

"And he was white, of course."

"Yeah, and he's dead."

Quiet settled through the car.

Tucker said, "You don't just walk into Roxbury looking for a black friend."

"That's what happens when you force all your black people to live in one place." Her voice was tinged with scorn.

"We don't force anyone to live anywhere."

"Anymore."

Tucker uncrossed his arms, crossed them the other way.

Dayna navigated off Sunset Boulevard, rising into the hills. "If you won't go to Roxbury, why would these guys fly all the way out here?"

"I guess 'cause they're racists from Boston," Tucker said, looking out the window.

"Don't be pissy. I'm saying there has to be something else."

"I don't know what it would be."

* * *

The good news was that Eddy didn't bother to "offer" Dayna another plum role on his sitcom. The bad news was that he wanted something else.

The three sat between Eddy's two infinity pools. He said, "All I'm asking is that you contact them and bring them to the oil field off Sepulveda."

Dayna didn't say anything. Eddy continued, "I'll take care of the rest."

That's what she was worried about. "If these guys killed Dagger, this is something for the police."

She'd mentioned the three guys when the officer questioned her at the party but she knew better than anyone that the LAPD wasn't always receptive to tips—especially since she admitted she hadn't actually seen any of the three men there. But still. "Why not go to the cops?"

Eddy gave her a look. "You're seriously wondering why I'm not going to the police. Really? I would've expected that from him." He motioned to Tucker, who winced. "Not you."

Dayna did not like his implication. At all. "I'm not telling you to invite them to your house for a game of Spades. But you need to let them know if there's something going on here. Unless you're hiding something."

"Because of course I'm the one who has to be the one hiding something. So much for looking out for each other, *sister*."

Dayna was about to give him her own nickname when Tucker spoke. "I'll do it."

He rose and left. Dayna decided to follow rather than fight, throwing Eddy one last look before leaving.

She didn't say anything until they were back in her car. "What's with the sudden action hero thing?"

Tucker shrugged.

Dayna said, "I'm not going."

"Don't worry. I'll take an Uber."

"Great. You and your *Uber* have a good time." She started the car. "Looks like you finally made a black friend."

The winter sun in Los Angeles, while bright and warm, doesn't last any longer than the winter sun in Boston. It had set before five, then the rain had started. None of them had planned for showers so they got wet in the dark.

Nickels, Ticky and Bob used their cellphones as flashlights as they walked along a primitive dirt road. Tucker used his phone as a GPS, finding the spot that Eddy had texted.

"They look like fucking dinosaurs," Nickels said, pointing at the oil pumps.

"Would you just shut up?" Ticky said.

"Fuck you."

"Fuck *you*."

"Why don't the two of you go fuck yourselves," Bob said, invoking a brilliant instance of mediation, Charlestown style.

"We're almost there," Tucker said as they approached an oil rig. Rain spattered down on them without conviction. "That's far enough," Eddy said, raising a rifle.

Except Eddy didn't say *far*. He said *fah*. In fact Eddy had lost any trace of the way he'd spoken last night or earlier that day. He'd suddenly developed a classic Charlestown accent.

Oh shit.

"What the fuck, Ed!" Bob said.

Nickels reached into his coat and Eddy shot him in the chest.

"What the *fuck*?" Eddy asked, pointing the rifle. "I should be asking *you* what the fuck."

"You screwed us, man," Ticky said, hands up, looking down at Nickels then back at Eddy. "We all went to jail but you got off because the cops were looking for four white guys and they thought you were black."

"Not my fault cops are stupid."

"Taking the money and screwing us was your fault," Bob said. "We want a share."

"I'll give you a share," Eddy said. He fired twice more, dropping Bob and Ticky. He pointed the rifle at Tucker and waved it. "There's a shovel over there."

Dayna had pulled to the side of the road on La Cienega, cursing Tucker, cursing Eddy, and cursing Mother Nature for the rain. Next to her, cars crept along the road. Angelenos treated every rainfall like a natural disaster.

When they had left Eddy's, Tucker had started fiddling with his

Uber app and Dayna had realized he was serious about bringing those Boston guys to the oil fields.

"I have a bad feeling about this," Dayna said.

"Four white guys, one black guy, of course you have a bad feeling," Tucker said.

Dayna bit down her response. Took a breath. "You've got nothing to prove."

"*I expect that from him*," Tucker mimicked Eddy.

"Fine," Dayna had said. If Tucker wanted to play action hero, she wanted him to have a happy ending. "At least let's set up Find Friends, so I know where you are."

Tucker had relented, and a little dot had appeared on a map on Dayna's phone.

Now the dot had moved deep into the oil field. That was bad.

She got out of the car, thanking "Past" Dayna for having the foresight not to wear heels. On the other hand, her sneakers were going to be ruined. Once out of the car, she assessed the situation. The rain wasn't bad so much as it was annoying. She moved off toward Tucker's GPS dot.

Tucker's Skecher slipped off the top of the wet shovel as he dug. His ankle caught the metal, tearing the skin.

"Son of a bitch!" Tucker said.

"Keep digging," Eddy said.

Clearly, Eddy had not done the math. There was no way Tucker was going to dig a deep enough hole to cover three bodies in one evening. Eddy would figure that out in an hour or two. Then what?

"So where did you grow up?" Tucker asked.

"I said shut up and dig," Eddy motioned with the rifle. "This ain't a fucking Boston reunion."

"We're going to be here a while. No harm telling me."

Eddy waited and then said, "Medford Street. They live on Chappie."

"*Lived*."

"What? Yeah."

Tucker got a hole dug about five inches deep. These would be shallow graves.

Tucker said, "You could have just paid them. Maybe sold one of the infinity pools."

"It wasn't the money," Eddy said.

"Right. This is about principle."

"This is about keeping a secret. The first time those assholes get drunk they'll be telling everyone that Eddy Washington, famous black man, is really Ed Gallagher, bank-robbing white guy. Next thing you know, I'm in prison."

"Well—"

"Also, I like having two infinity pools."

Dayna had been right. The sneakers were a complete loss. Still, she kept going, ignoring her wet socks. Part of her hoped they were all having a heart-to-heart worthy of a Christmas special. That way she could scream, maybe yell a bit, tell Tucker he had to pay if she got a parking ticket or worse, booted. But she knew better.

She alternated between looking at Tucker's little dot on her cell and looking for the real thing. The map app estimated she was five minutes away. She listened for voices, instead she heard a gunshot. Then a pause. Then two more gunshots.

She took off toward the sound. As she neared the Find Friends dot, she heard voices.

"...they'll be telling everyone that Eddy Washington, famous black man, is actually Ed Gallagher, bank-robbing white guy..."

Of course he was. Eddy had always sounded like a black guy written by a white screenwriter. Her first reaction was to run out there and smack Eddy in his stupid Ed Gallagher face. Then she saw the rifle, the bodies, and Tucker in the background digging.

She hid among some moldy ropes and other trash, dialed 9-1-1, and hoped the GPS would send the cops to the right place. She'd wait.

"Can't you dig any faster?" Eddy said to Tucker.

"I'm digging as fast as I can...Ed," Tucker said.

"This is going to take all night."

"Think of it as a word problem," Tucker said continuing to work the shovel. "If Tucker can dig a five-inch hole in fifteen minutes..."

"It's not worth burying you all." Eddy raised the rifle.

"I'll work faster."

Tucker's big mouth was about to get him killed. Dayna looked around at the trash, considered the rope, came up with a plan.

* * *

Ask an engineer about a *death march* and you'll hear about a project doomed by management's schedule. This grave-digging was no different. Tucker's only hope, despite his temper flare up, was to keep Ed focused on the graves. Otherwise Ed would cancel the project: *death march*.

Tucker's Apple watch tapped him on the wrist. He stopped digging, looked at it.

"Yeah, it's getting late," Eddy said. "This isn't going to work out."

The text was from Dayna: Look behind you.

Tucker blew out some air, pretending to be winded, looked over his shoulder. Saw light from an iPhone.

Another text tapped his wrist: Run to me!

Eddy said, "What the fuck are you doing? Dig!"

Tucker shook his head.

"No?" Eddy sounded pissed.

Tucker hesitated.

The watch tapped him again: "Trust me. I got this."

He didn't run, instead opting to fling a handful of dirt at Eddy. It caught him by surprise but only for a split second. He raised his rifle but only got it halfway before Tucker flung the shovel at him. It hit him square in the check. It was all the time Tucker needed to rush past him and reach Dayna.

Dayna said, "Go! Go! Keep running!"

Tucker did just that.

Eddy ran, holding his rifle, chasing Tucker. Just before he reached Dayna, she pulled hard on the rope she'd rigged. It sprang up six inches in a taut line, tripping Eddy. As he fell the rifle landed in the soft mud just out of his reach.

By the time Eddy looked up, Dayna held the rifle—pointed between his eyes.

Tucker walked up. "You shouldn't point a gun at someone you're not going to shoot."

"Exactly."

A police chopper buzzed overhead, its spotlight taking in the whole scene, its loudspeaker shouting instructions.

* * *

The saucer building of LAX loomed into view as Dayna pulled into the airport. It had been a good week for Tucker. He'd taken a Universal Studios tour, ridden the Ferris wheel in Santa Monica, and listened to music at Whiskey a Go Go.

Dayna had taken him shopping, doing some styling, and then brought him to some real Hollywood parties.

Tucker climbed out of the Infiniti and hoisted his bag.

"If you're ever in Boston..." Tucker told her.

"I'll let you know."

"You sure I can't pay for the ride? You *are* a Lyft driver after all."

"No, no," Dayna said. "What are friends for?"

This issue Jeff keeps up his fascinating stream of factual columns, this time focusing on one of the bestselling novelists of all times, Erle Stanley Gardner. Best known for his Perry Mason character, Gardner was also a lawyer in real life, instrumental in not only freeing innocent men from prison, but setting up his "Court of Last Resort" as a means for a group of influential people to help similarly innocent but convicted people of seeking justice. Most of us know Gardner as a writer, of course, but in addition to the Perry Mason books and long-lasting television show starring Raymond Burr, he was also not only an incredibly prolific contributor to pulp magazines but an enormously popular one as well. Gardner had many more characters than just Mason, including the Donald Lam and Bertha Cool series he wrote under the pseudonym "A.A. Fair." In this installment of Placed in Evidence, *Jeff takes us on an in-depth look at Gardner's books featuring District Attorney Doug Selby. Pay some good attention here. Gardner reached incredible heights for a reason, and the first entry in the Selby series is often cited as one of the best crime novels of its era...*

Placed in Evidence
Non-Fiction
J. Kingston Pierce

Erle Stanley Gardner was in a quandary. Even something of a snit. The year was 1936, and as crime writer/critic Dorothy B. Hughes recalls in her 1978 biography, *Erle Stanley Gardner: The Case of the Real Perry Mason*, Gardner was seriously entertaining the notion of phasing out Perry Mason as a protagonist.

By then, he'd already published nine novels featuring that Los Angeles criminal defense attorney; his younger secretary with the "perfect" legs, Della Street; and Paul Drake, the droop-shouldered private eye whose 24-hour investigative agency never seemed to find time for clients other than Mason. The books had sold well, allowing Gardner to end his own marginally satisfying legal career and become a full-time—and remarkably prolific—author. Hollywood had further promoted the series, with Warner Bros. adapting six Mason yarns for the silver screen in half as many years. However, Warners had recently decided not to renew its option on the character (its last Mason picture, *The Case of the Stuttering Bishop*, would be released during the summer of 1937), and Gardner had begun to quarrel with his publisher over the text and titles of his novels. In the midst of all this, explains Hughes, he was losing faith in his shrewd and determined advocate. His solution: to send Mason off on a trip to the Orient, never to return, and replace him with "a brand-new character, similar in many respects to Perry Mason, [only] a little more refined, a little less daring, a little more sophisticated."

As we all know, of course, Gardner eventually recovered from his spasm of pique, changed his mind about sending Perry packing,

and went on to feature him in a total of 82 novels before passing away in 1970, at age 80. But the author didn't meanwhile abandon his idea to create another series lead. In 1937, he added to his writing responsibilities the creation of a new succession of books starring Douglas Selby, the scrappy district attorney for fictional Madison County, California.

Introduced in 1937's *The D.A. Calls It Murder*, Selby faced off regularly against a colorful array of adversaries, including a buffoonish, headline-hunting chief of police and a smooth-talking but rascally L.A. attorney described as having "his finger in every unsavory pie in the county." Early reviewers applauded this second Gardner line of books for boasting "plenty of action," and greeted its star with great expectations; in its critique of *The D.A. Calls It Murder*, *The New York Times* observed that Selby, "like Mason, is a fighter who can take it as well as he can dish it out." Doug Selby was upright and earnest, distinctly human and—unlike Mason—

fallible. Yet he featured in a mere nine novels before vanishing (not in a China-bound ship). That was unfortunate, because while those stories never enjoyed the same level of reader enthusiasm Perry Mason's escapades did, and were neither as humorous nor as briskly paced as another series Gardner launched in 1939, built around mismatched L.A. gumshoes Bertha Cool and Donald Lam, they certainly offered plenty in the way of knotty plots, ill-starred suspects, and razzle-dazzle legal shenanigans.

When we first meet Doug Selby, he's just been elected to lead the District Attorney's Office in Madison City, a 90-year-old former cattle-ranching and mining community—still dependent on agriculture for much of its prosperity—located roughly 70 miles outside of L.A. Madison City is also the governmental seat of Madison County (based on Southern California's Ventura County, where Gardner lived and practiced law for many years, while concocting fiction at night). Selby, described as "a handsome young man with curly hair, a devil-may-care glint in his penetrating eyes, and a forceful, though shapely, mouth," won his new position after "a bitterly contested battle" against an unscrupulous, deeply entrenched incumbent D.A. named Sam Roper. Selby had run on a reform ticket together with the now county sheriff, Rex Brandon, a leathery-faced cattleman a quarter-century Selby's senior, whose legs are "bowed from years spent on horseback" and who boasts "a keen knowledge of human nature."

Selby figures that winning their campaign was the hardest thing the pair faced, and that thereafter they can get down to the business of administering evenhanded justice. But Brandon, who grew up in the area, warns Selby that their political opponents haven't gone away, and that they are destined to face now challenges from petty grifters and scoundrels moving in from the City of Angels. "[T]he main thing is," he says, "that we've got to watch our step, particularly at the start. If we make just one minor mistake, they'll hoot us out of office."

Crooks and out-of-power malcontents aren't the only ones likely to make their lives tough. *The Blade*, one of two local newspapers—closely allied with Sam Roper—demonstrates from the outset that it will take every opportunity to castigate Selby as incompetent, credulous, and callow. Fortunately, he and Brandon can count on better treatment from *The Madison County Clarion* and its rising-star reporter, Sylvia Martin, who's ready to lend Selby aid and feed him information in exchange for the inside line on his criminal investigations.

Like so many other mystery-fictionists of his era, Gardner was stingy with his characters' descriptions and back-stories. For instance, we learn little about Selby's history over nine books, except that he won a boxing championship in

college. It's not until halfway through the series that Sheriff Brandon's sturdy, no-nonsense wife (never given a forename) receives better than a passing mention. And the author's portrait of Sylvia Martin never extends much beyond her being an attractive, "trimly efficient," poised, and "spunky" young woman gifted with "a nose for sleuthing." To the best of my recollection, we're never told so much as that journalist's hair color, though the cover illustration on a 1946 Canadian paperback edition of *The D.A. Goes to Trial*—the fourth entry in this series—imagined her as a blonde.

One other thing we learn about Sylvia Martin: her relationship with Selby has the potential to become more than professional. They wind up dining together, traveling together in fervid pursuit of clues, and sharing small intimacies. Yet the workaholic Sylvia—like Della Street with a press pass—is reluctant to get closer to the man she works so closely with and clearly admires.

The American novelist, literary critic, and *Atlantic Monthly* editor William Dean Howells brooked no patience for "exaggerated" fiction designed to startle readers rather than make them "think and feel." He wrote disparagingly of stories with "a complicated plot, spiced with perils, surprises and suspenses." Which suggests he would have been apoplectic over Gardner's fiction, for it was distinguished by nothing so prominently as plot convolutions, bombshell revelations, and storytelling velocity.

Take, for example, *The D.A. Calls It Murder*. It finds Selby and

Brandon investigating a suspicious hotel death: The Reverend Charles Brower has perished in his room, ostensibly from an overdose of sleeping pills and a weak "ticker." But as it turns out, the deceased wasn't who he claimed to be, and his demise was well short of accidental. What's more, Brower left behind an envelope containing a mysterious $5,000, along with newspaper clippings about a movie starlet (who just happened to be hiding out in the same hotel) and a lawsuit over the proper disposal of a fat estate. While *The Blade* demands expeditious results, Selby and Brandon are confronted with the puzzle of a poisoned watchdog, an evidently impossible set of photographs, and an interview with a dead man.

In another writer's hands, these assorted leads and red herrings might have resulted in a mess. But Gardner was deft at juggling such volatile ingredients, even if—as in this case—leaps of faith must be executed and a confession heard in order to make sense of them all. One interesting twist here, to be echoed in later series entries, is to see Selby periodically caught flat-footed, his trusting nature exploited by folks with nefarious agendas. There are never doubts that Selby will triumph in the end, but unlike the more confident, imperturbable Perry Mason, he often depends on the intervention of supporters such as Sylvia Martin to ensure that happening.

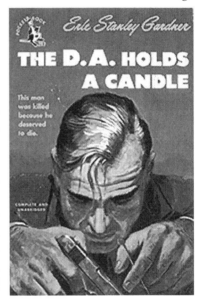

The Selby tales became no less intricately structured or propulsive as their numbers multiplied. Book two, *The D.A. Holds a Candle* (1938), has the district attorney and sheriff dealing, in part, with the auto camp death of a hitchhiker. The man appears to have succumbed to carbon monoxide poisoning, caused by a faulty gas heater left running in his room on a cold night. However, there are some peculiar aspects to this tragedy, including that the deceased was huddled behind a dresser with a gun in his hand and a prolix note indicating he was lying in wait for somebody else—somebody the note insists "deserved to die." Did this wayfarer's presumably accidental demise prevent another person's murder? Meanwhile, there's a gambling racket to uncover, a hit-and-run incident that requires probing, and a pompous capitalist—the father of Inez Stapleton, Sylvia Martin's rival for Selby's affections—to mollify. As is so frequently true in these stories, the cases Selby, Brandon, and Sylvia Martin tackle wind up linking together in unpredictable ways.

In 1939's *The D.A. Draws a Circle*, a resident in one of Madison City's pricier corners, Rita Artrim, makes a late-night phone call to

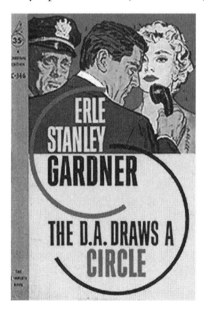

the police, saying she's spotted a naked prowler scurrying along the edge of a deep, narrow ravine adjacent to her property. That same night, a pistol shot is heard in the area. The city's police chief, Otto Larkin—a paunchy, thickheaded "political stooge" in his early 30s who's wont to take credit for successes that aren't his and eschews blame when things go awry—dismisses the alleged gunfire as insignificant. But upon investigation, the unclothed corpse of a man is discovered in the canyon. He's been shot twice, with both bullets fired from different guns yet having traveled through the selfsame hole. Equally odd is evidence showing one bullet was fired directly into the victim's nude flesh, while the other passed initially through fabric. As if all of that weren't enough to test Selby's deductive skills, throw in an elusive bail-jumper, strange doings in the Antrim household, a possible insurance scam, and the disappearance of Rita Antrim's father-in-law—reportedly debilitated by an accident that's also said to have left him with amnesia.

The D.A. Draws a Circle adds to this series' mix of regular players one Alphonse Baker Carr, a tall, suave, big-time criminal lawyer from L.A. in his mid-50s, known to his customarily questionable clients as "Old A.B.C." He claims to have taken up residence in

Madison City for the purpose of retirement, but never quite gets around to trimming his practice. Appearing in all but one of the remaining six Selby books, Carr is a richly comic figure with a malleable code of ethics: he'll do pretty much anything to get his clients off. Just as prone as Perry Mason is to capitalize on legal loopholes, Carr is very much like the dark side of Gardner's most famous attorney. The more straightforward Selby appreciates Carr as a legal "artist," but doesn't trust him. With good reason.

Being among the best of these yarns, it's understandable that *The D.A. Draws a Circle* was adapted (loosely) into a Doug Selby TV pilot. Gardner had been trying for years to launch such a show, but the two-hour, 1971 NBC film retitled *They Call It Murder* was as close as he got. Scripted by *Have Gun—Will Travel* creator Sam Rolfe, the pilot starred Jim Hutton (later to give a superior performance in the 1975-1976 mystery drama *Ellery Queen*), with Lloyd Bochner as a particularly oleaginous Carr. Sadly, Gardner died before *They Call It Murder* premiered, and NBC declined to turn it into a weekly program.

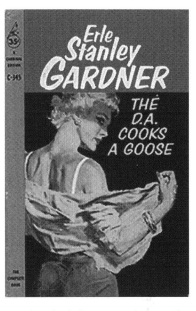

By 1939, Gardner had his writing hands full. Not only was he turning out two Perry Mason books per annum, but he'd also just published—under the pseudonym A.A. Fair—*The Bigger They Come*, the first of what would ultimately be 30 Cool and Lam novels.

Nonetheless, he continued penning Doug Selby books, if at a slightly reduced clip. 1940 saw the release of *The D.A. Goes to Trial*, which involves a dead hobo of dubious identity; an absconding wife and a suspect divorce; ill-matched fingerprints and embezzlement; plus the return of Inez Stapleton, who's won a legal degree in hopes that Selby will take her more seriously. In *The D.A. Cooks a Goose* (1942)—another high-water mark for this series—we're given a no-less-bewildering amalgam of plot elements, among them a hit-and-run accident that injured a woman and killed her baby; another infant, found at a bus depot; a supposedly confirmed bachelor with a secret spouse and an unexpected fortune; and a too-convenient last will and testament. Another two years passed before the debut of *The D.A. Calls a Turn* (1944).

It sees Selby and Brandon responding to a desperate call from a  man who says he's drunk and in possession of a stolen vehicle. The pair arrive on the scene too late, though: the man is killed in a traffic accident, leaving our heroes to figure out why he was dressed as a vagrant, yet had professionally manicured fingernails and handmade shoes. It doesn't take long for the corpse to be identified as that of a chain store grocer, and for an autopsy to reveal that he actually perished *before* the car crash. A long-ago prison riot, a conniving wife, and another instance of memory loss all heighten the mystery.

While their plot lines ripple with issues of jurisprudence, the Selby books are as much traditional detective stories as they are legal mysteries. The D.A. continually demonstrates the depths of his deductive acumen—and often gambles his reputation on smart guesswork. Also on display in these tales is Gardner's appreciation for California's rural reaches and the simpler ways of its people, all of which are endangered by spreading cities. He writes of citrus-tree growers combating frost with "smudge smoke which lay as a black pall over the community"; of parched November days when "hillsides [were] seamed and fissured with heat cracks"; and of "the hoarse bark of tractors as ranchers, bundled against the cold, pulled plows across the fertile soil." Many Selby yarns were syndicated in *The Country Gentleman*, an American agricultural magazine, and it's easy to understand their appeal to that audience.

Gardner wanted his Perry Mason novels to remain as timeless as possible, so he minimized references to historical events. On the other hand, he sent his "brainy little runt" of a series shamus, Donald Lam, off to fight the Japanese during World War II; and in *The D.A. Breaks a Seal* (1946), we learn Doug Selby has resigned his office to enlist in the Army, working in counterespionage. But for this story, *Major* Selby is on a five-day furlough and back in Madison City, just in time to help tackle the puzzle of a lone hotel guest who was poisoned after having *two* breakfasts sent to his room, and aid Inez Stapleton in contesting a dead woman's will.

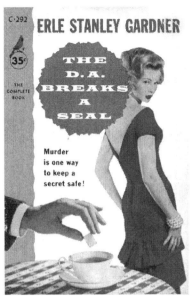

The concluding pair of books in this line—best read in order of their publication—find Selby out of uniform again and returned to the District Attorney's Office, after a "nasty fight" that nearly led to his replacement's recall. *The D.A.*

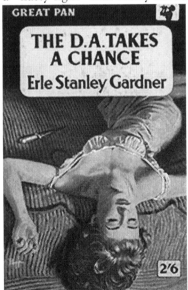

Takes a Chance (1948) embroils Gardner's protagonist in the bizarre story of a house party gone wrong, which may or may not have resulted in shots being fired, but was definitely followed by the sequestering of a fetching "Hollywood party girl"...who is soon after murdered, allegedly by a carving knife bearing Sheriff Brandon's prints. A.B. Carr's manipulation of people and alibis here almost proves his undoing, and desperate measures are required to save him from criminal prosecution and disbarment. Municipal corruption forms a background to this story, reminding readers that Selby and Brandon must occasionally walk a delicate political path to maintain their jobs. Finally, in *The D.A. Breaks an Egg* (1949), we discover *The Blade* under new but equally hostile management, ready to denounce Selby

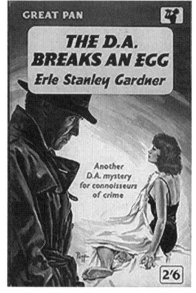

and Brandon over their handling of an inquiry that involves a stolen car, a bilked gambler, a corpse in a park, a baffling burglary, a female private eye who "specializes on cases involving playboys," and a murder victim who turns out to be very much alive. Once more, Carr's maneuverings leave him precariously positioned, but there's every chance he'll escape indictment and remain free to torment the D.A. and the sheriff, as well as newshound Sylvia Martin, who by the end of this book appears to have captured Selby's romantic notice. (It's about time!)

So why, when there still seemed many inviting avenues down which this series might travel, did Erle Stanley Gardner cut it off at nine books? Jeffrey Marks, the director of development at publisher Crippen & Landru, and author of an as-yet-unpublished Gardner biography, suggests Gardner was too busy with his Mason series, his Cool and Lam books, a weekday Mason radio drama, and other endeavors to spare time for Selby. "The gap between each book," Marks says, had grown to "18 months, which displeased Gardner, since he couldn't remember the characters and details that long. Finally, he just gave up on [Selby], contenting himself with two best-selling series."

The result? Seven decades after Doug Selby's last outing, Perry Mason is a household name. Cool and Lam are being rediscovered, thanks to publisher Hard Case Crime. And Selby is all but forgotten.

Here we are at the featured story for this issue, by Walter Satterth-wait, a writer who many describe with that somewhat vague label, "a writer's writer." Walter started his writing career with short stories, very good short stories, that were later gathered in two collectible editions. He's written both series books—featuring PI Joshua Croft—as well as standalones, and notably novels featuring historical characters, like Oscar Wilde, Harry Houdini, and two with "Miss Lizzie," the infamous Lizzie Borden. Perhaps Walter simply didn't write enough books to crack the ranks of bestsellerdom and reach the level of mass market success he probably should have, but I think it can safely be said that Walter's work has always been very much appreciated by his peers. In 1993 Ernie Bulow published a book called, Sleight of Hand: Conversations with Walter Satterthwait, *and I can't think of a much bigger compliment than a book like that. His book* Dead Horse, *a "fictional" retelling of the death (suicide? Murder?) of hard-boiled pioneer and pulp writing star Raoul Whitfield, is a must-read and will be republished by Stark House Books later this year. Enjoy this story. I truly hope it won't be the last, but you never know. The world keeps turning for all of us, doesn't it?*

The Death of Mr. Jayacody
Walter Satterthwait

Bhante had gone to bed early tonight, at ten o'clock. At ten-thirty, Fallon began cleaning up the jetsam left by the slow steady surge of the day.

It was at precisely ten-fifty-five, in the garage, while he was wheeling the big black garbage barrel alongside the ancient Toyota Land Cruiser and toward the broad double roll-down door, that he noticed the door was already separated from the concrete floor by two or three inches. He glanced to the left, around the rear of the Cruiser, and discovered, seemingly pinned there by the bottom of the door, the head of Mr. Jayacody.

The door lay directly across his throat. Fallon jerked the big plastic barrel upright, turned and slammed his palm against the red button on the control unit that opened the door. As the door lurched up, Fallon stepped over to Mr. Jayacody, squatted down and slipped his fingertips along the neck, looking for a pulse. Mr. Jayacody didn't have one.

The man's flesh was cooling. Gently, Fallon probed along the curvatures of his throat. Mr. Jayacody's larynx had been crushed.

Fallon felt over the man's head, under his thicket of white, perfectly crew-cut hair. He found a small soft lump on the back of his skull.

He stood, wiped his hands on his sweatpants, looked over at his motorcycle on the right, shrouded in its gray canvas rain cover. The bike was probably okay. He looked up and ran his glance along the door opener's electric container box, and along the cabling and the thick rubber belt that connected it to the door. Everything there seemed okay as well. There were switches at the rear of the box that adjusted high point and low point of the door's position, but getting up there was a bit of a nuisance—dancing the ladder around the garage always produced a bout of bitter slapstick.

He examined the floor near Mr. Jayacody's head. Footprints in the dust, but faint and smeared. In the spillover from the ceiling's large bright light, he examined the paved driveway on which the rest of Mr. Jayacody was lying, his arms flung out, both his legs bent and twisted to one side. He was wearing a three-piece grey suit with a soft pin-striping, black socks, and a pair of shiny black quarter-brogue shoes. Mr. Jayacody had always dressed well.

The black leather of the shoes was powdered with dust.

Fallon stepped over and examined the round red sensors that were designed to detect movement within the doorway, to make sure the door didn't bang into something—or someone—moving into the garage or out of it.

The sensors had been unclipped from their usual position and raised to a new one, some two or three inches higher.

Fallon glanced at his watch. Eleven-oh-five. Time to wake up Bhante and call the cops.

"All right, all *right*," came the sleepy voice from inside Bhante's room, a bit muffled by the door.

"Bhante," Fallon said, keeping his own voice low. The three

monks-in-training slept in rooms along the hallway behind him. "We need to talk," he said. "Right now."

"Yes, yes. Come in."

Fallon opened the door, flicked the light switch.

"Argh!" said Bhante and threw up his arm as the overhead light popped on. Naked, he was sitting with his back against the headboard, his knees raised beneath the sheet, which was drawn up over his waist. Blinking rapidly, he waved his right hand in front of his round young face, back and forth. "No light!" he said in what was supposed to be a whisper but wasn't. His bare brown upper arm furiously wobbled. "No *light*!"

"Wrong," Fallon said. "No. We need it."

Blinking away, Bhante said, "*Why?*" He waved his hand some more, to demonstrate that he was still serious about the light.

"Because Mr. Jayacody is dead," Fallon told him.

The hand dropped to the sheet and Bhante cocked his head. "What?"

"Mr. Jayacody is dead. Outside. Well, partly outside."

Bhante drew the sheet up over his chest and held it against himself. "Partly? Partly dead?"

"Partly outside, partly in the garage. Totally dead."

Bhante ran his hand over the top of his shiny bald scalp, from back to front. He blinked some more. "How did this happen, Phil? Are you certain he is dead?"

"Very certain. I don't know how it happened."

"A heart attack?"

"I don't think so. We need to call the cops."

He frowned again, sadly, his bare brown shoulders sinking. "Oh no, Phil. The police? Why the police?"

"There's a law, Bhante. Someone dies on your property, you call the cops."

"Yes, yes. Of course. I knew that." He looked away, scowling, and then blew out a big puff of air. "But I do not like the police."

"This is your library?" asked Detective Breedlove as the two of them walked into the room.

"That's right," said Fallon.

It was a large room in the large house. Three easy chairs, one comfortable sofa, a long coffee table, three walls filled with tall bookcases, most of these dense with dark, old, hard-covered books. Over in the corner was a cushioned antique love seat. Long golden curtains covered the wide double windows.

Fallon was carrying a tray that held a white china teapot, two thick white china mugs, a small stack of wooden coasters, a few folded paper napkins, a small white bowl of sugar, a small white pitcher of milk, and a pair of silver-plated spoons. Very domestic.

He said, "Have a seat on the sofa, Detective. This end, please."

As Breedlove side-stepped between the sofa and the coffee table, Fallon laid the tray on the table and organized the tea settings along the table's top.

Breedlove sat down on the sofa.

"Milk and sugar," Fallon said, nodding to the china on the tray. He lifted the pot and poured the detective some tea, then poured some for himself, then lowered the teapot back onto the tray. He sat down in the big easy chair opposite the sofa.

Breedlove said, "So this is an actual monastery?"

"Yes," said Fallon. "Recognized as a legal place of worship by the city, state, and federal governments." He raised his mug. "Cheers."

The detective leaned forward, lifted his own mug but didn't tap it against Fallon's. "Right." He took a small quick sip, then set the mug down. "Interesting taste. What is that?"

"Ceylon green tea."

"Interesting. Okay, Mr. Fallon. You ready to answer some questions?"

Smiling, holding the mug in his lap, Fallon leaned back. "Raring to go, Detective."

"Right," said Breedlove. From the left inside pocket of his sportcoat he plucked a small flat electronic voice recorder and set it on the table. From his right inside pocket he plucked a flip-cover notebook and a ball point pen. Keeping the notebook and pen in his left hand, he reached out to the voice recorder and pushed one of its small silver buttons. He turned the recorder's face toward himself, peered at its digital display, gave a small, satisfied nod, and then laid it back on the table. He sat back, opening the notebook. "What's your full name, Mr. Fallon?"

"Phillip Fallon."

"Middle name?"

"I don't use one."

"But you have one."

"Yes I do."

Breedlove waited to hear it, but Fallon merely smiled at him politely.

Finally Breedlove said, "So what is it?"

"Oh. Sorry. Michael."

"Okay." Breedlove announced this to the air around him while keeping an eye on Fallon. "This is Detective Roger Breedlove interviewing Mr. Phillip Fallon on the premises of The Spring Dawn Meditation Center. The time is—" he glanced at his watch, "—twelve-oh-five a.m. All right, Mr. Fallon. Suppose you tell me what happened earlier tonight. Start at the beginning."

Fallon took a sip of tea. "At just before eleven, I was—"

"That's eleven p.m., correct?"

"Tonight, you said. Well, last night now. But it was still p.m."

"Right. Only clarifying."

"Right," said Fallon. He took another sip of tea. "At just before eleven p.m., I was taking the garbage out through the garage and I found Mr. Jayacody lying under the garage door. All I could see was his head. I pushed the button—"

"The light was on but the garage door was closed?"

"The overhead garage light was on. That isn't connected to the door. When we got the system, the two lights that're built into the door-opener kept shorting out, first one, then the other. It was a pain to fix. Moving the Toyota, schlumping out the ladder, climbing up the damn thing, screwing two bulbs out, screwing two bulbs in—it was annoying. Since I'm the only one who goes into the garage, and since not having the lights doesn't bother me, I stopped replacing the bulbs. I've got a flashlight."

Breedlove grinned. "You don't like heights."

Fallon smiled. "No. Not much."

"Who installed the door opener?"

"I did."

"Why not use the warranty and get a new one?"

"The opener was a gift from one of the members. He delivered it here himself. If I got a new one, I'd have to get a different one. Another model—I didn't trust the old one. If he ever came into the garage, he'd see the new one and he'd get upset. I didn't want him to get upset. It's a Buddhist thing, Detective. And, as I said, not having those two lights doesn't bother me."

"Okay. Let's get back on track. You saw Mr. Jayacody's head. Then what?"

"I pressed the button on the control unit that opens and closes the door manually. The door opened and I checked on Mr. Jayacody. He was dead and he was—"

"There's a remote for the door?"

"Two of them. I keep one in my jacket, which is in the closet in my room, which is locked, and one in the glove compartment of the Toyota, which is also locked. The button on the wall was closer than either of those."

"Did you check on them?"

"The remotes? Before I talked to Bhante. They were both where they were supposed to be."

"Mr. Jayacody was dead, you said. How did you know?"

"He had no pulse and he was already growing cold. I went back into the monastery and spoke to the abbot, Bhante Dhammika, and I told him we had to call the police. He understood. So I did that— called the police—and about ten minutes later a couple of Tampa officers showed up, and then an ambulance."

"You ever get any medical training, Mr. Fallon?"

"No."

"But you touched the body?"

Again, Fallon smiled politely. "I just said I did, Detective."

"Only clarifying, Mr. Fallon."

Fallon nodded. "Right."

Detective Breedlove said, "You ever touch a dead body before this one?"

"Yes."

"Uh huh. And when did that occasion arise?"

"That occasion arose during the Gulf War. Several times."

The detective raised his hand. "Right. Like I say, Mr. Fallon, only clarifying." He glanced very briefly at the voice recorder, looked back at Fallon. "Sorry for any losses you suffered there."

Fallon took another sip of tea. "Yeah," he said. "Thanks."

"Let's go back a little," said Breedlove.

"Sure."

"What exactly was the victim doing here?"

"You've decided he was a victim?"

The detective flatly recited: "The two officers determined that there was a good possibility of foul play and they requested detectives from the Homicide Unit where Foster and me were next in line. It's our job to determine if the officers were right and if so, to determine who was responsible for Mr. Jayacody's death. As you know, Detective Foster is interviewing Banty. I'm interviewing you. You mind if I'm the one who asks the questions here, Mr. Fallon?"

Smiling again, Fallon shook his head slightly. He sipped at his tea. "Absolutely not," he said. "But it's *Bhante*, by the way, not *Banty*." He spelled it. "It's a Pali word. The English equivalent would be *Reverend*. Like Reverend Jim Jones or Reverend Jim Bakker."

Breedlove considered him. "You got something against Christian preachers, Mr. Fallon?"

"Not at all, Detective. Those are just the first reverends who sprang to mind."

The detective studied him for another moment, then said, "Why was Mr. Jayacody here, Mr. Fallon?"

"He was attending our Meditation Night. We do that four times a week. Monday, Wednesday, Friday, and Sunday. It's open. Everyone is invited, anyone can come. We start at seven in the Meditation Hall. P.M. Bhante gives a small talk, about half an hour's worth. Then we do a sitting meditation. That usually takes about twenty minutes. Then we do walking meditation in the back of the monastery. There are paths in the lawn and pathways through the woodland area. We've got lights in the trees, so no one gets lost. That takes another half an hour. Not everyone does it. Some of them stay inside and do more sitting meditation."

"How many of them stayed last night?"

"Seven or eight. Plus the three monks-in-training and Bhante. And I."

"The monks don't do the walking?"

"The monks and Bhante have been doing it all day long, off and on. They usually sit this one out."

"And you?"

"I've got a note from my mother."

Breedlove lowered his notebook. He frowned slightly. "This is a murder investigation, Mr. Fallon. Could we hold off on the jokes?"

Fallon showed the palm of his hand. "Sure."

"You didn't walk because...?"

"Because I didn't want to."

"That's allowed?"

"This isn't a prison, Detective."

Breedlove frowned again. With his pen, he quickly shooed away an invisible insect. "Okay," he said. "Back on track. The people walking. How do they know when their time is up?"

"Bhante opens the back door of the Meditation Hall and rings the temple bell. You can hear it from anywhere on the property."

"How many people were here total?"

"Twenty or so. With one exception, all the people who did the walking meditation came back to the hall."

"Mr. Jayacody was the exception."

"Right. I'll give you a list of names and addresses when we're done."

Breedlove nodded. "A list would be good. Okay. Did Mr. Jayacody arrive on time tonight?"

"A couple of minutes before seven. Along with the others."

"Just what kind of a name is Jayacody?"

"Sri Lankan. About a third of our members are Sri Lankan. Bhante Dhammika is Sri Lankan. This monastery is a branch of the Mother Monastery in Sri Lanka."

"They call it the Mother Monastery?"

"I call it the Mother Monastery. Bhante gets a bit upset when I do."

"Sri Lanka is over there by India, right?"

"Next door. Off the southeast coast."

The detective looked briefly down at his notebook, then looked back at Fallon. "Okay. So after the walking thing, do the people come back to the Meditation Hall and say, like, good night or whatever?"

"A lot of them do. But it's not required. Bhante explains all this before he sends them out. Some of the members have night-time jobs, some have babysitters. Some just slip away. But some of them have questions to ask, and Bhante hangs around to answer them."

"Hold on a second. The walking people, they can all get back to their cars without being seen by you or Bhante?"

"Sure. They've already got their shoes on. They can go around the house, on the side opposite of the garage. There's a passage between the bushes there. And on the front side, there's a slated pathway that runs along the edge of the lawn. They all park a block down the street, at the lot for the elementary school."

"You got permission for that?"

Fallon smiled, took a sip of tea. "We asked the school for permission and they gave it. It keeps the street clear for any kind of emergency vehicle. And it's one of the reasons we built the pathway. There's a branch of it that runs to the front door. Coming from the parking lot, most of the members walk on that. And they walk back the same way. Bhante and I can't see or hear them."

"But there's another pathway," said Breedlove. "Along the driveway. And Mr. Jayacody was lying there. If a member walked along that, wouldn't he see Mr. Jayacody at the garage door?"

"No. Most of the driveway is separated from the path by bushes, except a yard or so from the garage door. And my bike was parked exactly in that spot. Normally—"

"That your bike under the canvas?"

"Yeah."

"What kind?"

"A BMW."

"Nice bike. I got a Harley."

"Nice bike." He smiled. "Are we bonding, Detective?"

The detective prodded the air with his notebook. "Go ahead. Normally?"

"Normally I keep the bike in the garage, but on garbage nights I leave it out so I can maneuver the big garbage barrel out onto the driveway."

"What if someone came up and looked over the top of the bike, to the driveway?"

Fallon smiled. "Who's going to do that? The members all know that they can't get into the house from the garage. And besides, even if someone came up to the bike, there was no light showing through at the bottom of the door. And there was no moon last night. It's completely dark in that part of the driveway. Not that Mr. Jayacody minded."

Breedlove frowned faintly again. "Seems like you're taking his death pretty casually, Mr. Fallon."

"As I said, Detective, I didn't know him very well. I'm sorry he's dead, but I'm sorry when anybody dies."

His lips tightly closed, Breedlove nodded. "Uh huh." He looked down at his notebook. "Okay. The door wasn't halfway open before the meeting?"

"It was never halfway open. As I said, it was open maybe two or three inches when I found it at just before eleven." He added, "P.M."

With his pen, Breedlove lightly flicked away another invisible insect. "But was it open like that before the meeting started?"

"No."

"You're sure?"

"Positive."

"Why positive?"

"I was in there at around six-forty-five, tossing stuff into the trash barrel."

The detective wrote something in his notebook. He looked up. "Okay. So was Mr. Jayacody a regular here?"

"No. This was only his third visit. He came last week, Wednesday, for the first time, and then again on Friday. He didn't show up on Sunday."

"He have any problems with the other members of the group?"

"I wouldn't say that he had problems with them."

"What would you say?"

"I'd say that they had problems with him. I can't really speak for them, of course, but I think they mostly felt that Mr. Jayacody was a bit strange."

"Strange how?"

"He dressed formally all three times he came here. Suit and tie, polished shoes. Sri Lankans can be very formal, but not here, not in a meditation meeting. You need comfortable clothes to meditate. And he preferred being called *Mister* Jayacody by the rest of the group. He didn't like being addressed by his first name. The rest of the Sri Lankan members all use first names."

"You know his first name?"

"Kosala. I'll get his address and phone number for you when we're done."

Breedlove was writing in his notebook. "Yeah, good." He looked up. "Did Bhante call him by his last name?"

"His first name. Standard protocol with a head monk and a civilian. Unless the civilian is an elder."

"What kind of work did he do? Mr. Jayacody."

"Commodities, he told me. Futures. Beans, corn."

"Risky business." He wrote in the notebook.

"So I hear," said Fallon.

"He have any friends in the group?"

"No one knew him. Which is unusual. All the other Sri Lankan members know each other. He had only moved to Florida a couple of weeks ago, he told me."

"From where?"

"Originally from Sri Lanka, as I said. He moved to the States five years ago, but not to Florida."

"Where to?"

"He said he lived up north for a while. He didn't say where."

"Up north in the United States?"

Fallon shrugged. "Or Canada."

"You never asked him to be more specific?"

Fallon smiled. "I'm not a policeman, Detective."

"Probably a good thing."

"Probably."

Breedlove frowned. "You got something against cops, Mr. Fallon?"

Fallon laughed. "No."

Breedlove raised an eyebrow. "That a funny question?"

"In context, yeah. Sorry."

"Right." He stared at Fallon for a moment. Then he looked down at the notebook, looked back up. "So you don't know if he was married, divorced, widowed."

"No. He never said he had a partner. Every time he showed up here, he was alone."

"How did he know about your group, your meetings?"

"He found us online, he said. We run announcements on our web site, and we're linked all over the 'net. Buddhist groups, meditation groups."

"Okay." Breedlove flipped over a page and started a new one. "Now, Mr. Fallon, did you notice anything else in the garage?"

"I noticed that someone had moved the sensors on the garage door's railing a few inches higher. Three inches, I'd say."

Breedlove nodded. "They're on clips."

"Right."

"You unclip them and you can move them up or down."

"Right."

"And they were definitely moved."

"When I found Mr. Jayacody, yes."

"And they weren't moved when you were in there at six-forty-five?"

"No."

"Did you check the high and low adjustment switches on the control box?"

"No time. I was dealing with one dead member and four live monks."

"And you don't like heights."

Fallon smiled. "And I don't like heights. But checking them is probably a good idea."

Breedlove nodded. "So to you, all this signifies what?"

"It signifies that somebody wanted the door to stop moving downward when it was two or three inches from the floor."

"Why would somebody want that?"

"If the door hadn't been futzed with, it would have kept trying to get to the floor, but straight through Mr. Jayacody's neck. If it did, it might break apart the man's spinal column, but it might also break apart the whole garage door. I saw that happen once—it sounded like a pistol shot. And that would probably draw more attention than I think he wanted."

"More than this unidentified person wanted."

"That's right."

"It's possible Mr. Jayacody did it himself."

"Possible, sure," said Fallon. "But I doubt it."

Breedlove waited a moment and then said, "How come?"

"It's not very reliable, is it? There's no guarantee that it'll work, that it'll actually kill you. Maybe you screwed up with arranging the height of the door from the floor, maybe you didn't align your body properly with the door."

Detective Breedlove smiled. "How would *you* do it, Mr. Fallon?"

"Hypothetically? As a murderer? If I wanted to bring the garage door into the story?"

"Right."

"We agreed I'm not a policeman, Detective."

"Yeah, but you're a pretty sharp guy. I'd like to get your input."

Fallon laughed. "You'd like to find out if I'm a viable suspect. Detective, I was in a room with at least ten other people when Mr.

Jayacody was killed."

"If he was killed when you say."

"That's the only window. There's no other time he could've been killed."

"Maybe so. But I'm serious, Mr. Fallon." He made his face go serious, which didn't require much work. "I'd like to hear what you think. If you were the murderer, how would you do it?"

"I have a feeling this won't be very productive."

"Let's just give it a shot."

Fallon sipped at his tea. "Sure. The first thing I do, as soon as the walking meditation starts, is I meet Mr. Jayacody outside, on the back lawn. We agree to meet again at the garage. Or maybe the garage is where the two of them usually met."

"So you're the murderer and you're meeting Mr. Jayacody. Why are you supposed to be meeting him?"

"No idea, Detective. Something illegal. Drugs, maybe. Human trafficking. I don't know."

"Go ahead."

"There's a second back door into the monastery, just around the corner from this room. I don't have to come back in through the Meditation Hall. I can come back in through the second door. So I do that and I go down through the living room, past the laundry room, and into the garage. I turn on the garage light and look around for a weapon. I see a nice hoe hanging on the wall. Its handle is about the same thickness as the bottom rim of a garage door. I turn off the light. I open the garage door manually with the button on the control unit, to the left of the door."

"Why turn off the light?"

"Anyone driving by can see anyone standing in the garage."

"You couldn't hear the garage door open? From inside the house?"

"It's a pretty good door opener. Quiet. Belt driven, not chain. Nylon rollers, torsion springs, rubber buffers. I keep it lubricated and tightened up. And the Meditation Hall is soundproofed."

"Could any of the walkers have heard it? Outside?"

"I doubt it. As I said, it's a good machine, and there's a lot of greenery out back that muffles any kind of sound."

"Okay. So Mr. Jayacody comes down to the garage and meets you."

"Right. We talk for a bit. I suggest he look behind him. He does. I sap him or I sand-sock him."

"How do you know about sand-socks, Mr. Fallon?"

"I read a lot," said Fallon.

The detective shook his head. "Nah. A real sap is better. Leather and lead. Here in Florida you can buy 'em legal at any flea market—cash, no record."

"Swell. So I use a real sap. He goes down. I arrange the unconscious body, putting his throat exactly where the door would hit it. I can tell that from the metal strip along the floor."

"No light."

"Flashlight. I go over to the hoe, grab it, bring it back to the unconscious body, set the flashlight on the floor so I can clearly see his neck, I brace myself, and then I slam the handle down, hard as I can, on the man's throat. I wipe off the handle with a rag and I hook the hoe back on the wall. Then I close the door onto Mr. Jayacody's throat, check that it looks okay. I go from the garage back into the house."

He took a sip of his tea. "Then I have a choice. I can go out the front door and off to my car. Or I can go out the second back door, onto the back lawn and hang out there. Walk along one of the walkways until Bhante rings the monastery bell. Then go back into the house with everyone else. If it were me, that's what I do."

"So you look less like a suspect."

"Right. And that's what he did. Because they all came back." He leaned forward, set his cup down, lifted the teapot and poured himself some more tea. "Tea, Detective?"

"Huh? Oh, no thanks. I'm not really a big tea guy."

Fallon took a sip from his mug. "Are we about done here?"

"Just a couple of personal questions, Mr. Fallon. You mind?"

He smiled. "I guess we'll find out. But first, can I go use the toilet?"

"Naturally. I'll wait right here."

Fallon smiled. "Great," he said.

"All ready again, Mr. Fallon?"

Sitting back down in the big easy chair, Fallon said, "I'm aces, Detective."

Breedlove leaned forward, turned his voice recorder on again, and sat back against the sofa's cushions. "Right. Let's get your living situation straight. You live here on a full-time basis, is that right?"

"Mostly." Fallon picked up his mug of tea, sipped at it, sat back in the chair.

"Mostly?" said Breedlove.

"I have a house over in Dunedin."

"The address?"

Fallon gave it.

Writing in his notebook, Breedlove asked, "But you stay here every night?"

"Pretty much. Once every three weeks I spend a weekend over there."

"Why?"

"In a monastery, the lay people—which I'm one of—are supposed to keep the Five Precepts. Those are basically rules against lying, killing, stealing, doing drugs or alcohol, and sexual misconduct."

"This house is officially a monastery."

"Right. We established that, Detective."

"Only clarifying." He put a concerned look on his face. "You seem a little prickly, Mr. Fallon."

"A bit tired, maybe. Past my bedtime."

"So what do you do, over there in Dunedin?"

"Oh you know. The usual. A little rape. A little pillage."

Breedlove nodded. "And that's the answer you want on the recorder?"

Fallon smiled. "Okay. Once in a while, I like a beer with my pizza."

"A beer."

"And sometimes, afterward, a cocktail while I watch HBO. A cold Eagle Rare bourbon and water. This is all necessary, is it, Detective?"

"Yeah. The point is, you have no employment over there, correct?"

"Correct."

"This house," said Breedlove, "the one we're in. Who owns it?"

"The monastery pays the mortgage. They employ me."

"And what is it, exactly, you do here, Mr. Fallon? Bhante said you were in charge."

"Bhante was exaggerating. I'm only a steward."

"A steward?"

"There's one full monk here—the abbot, Bhante Dhammika—

and there are three men training as monks. None of those four is allowed to handle money or cook food or drive a car. Whatever they can't do, I do for them."

"You're like a...what?"

"Like a steward. Like Sir Kay at the Round Table. King Arthur handled all the kingly stuff, and he had a steward to handle all the other stuff. Logistics. Food, transport. That was Sir Kay. That's me."

"And Bhante is King Arthur."

"Exactly."

"A steward, huh?"

Fallon nodded. "It's a technical term."

"Uh huh. And how long have you been a steward?"

"About two years." He took another sip of his tea.

"And what were you doing before that?"

"For a long time I ran a bar."

"Over in Dunedin?"

"Over in Greece."

Breedlove nodded, his eyebrows lightly raised. "Greece the country."

"The island of Kos. In the eastern Aegean, close to Turkey."

"How long you do that for?"

"About ten years."

"And then what?"

"I had a partner, a Greek, and we sold the place to an Italian company. We did very well. I came back to the States four years ago, bought the house in Dunedin. Then, for a couple of years, I traveled around the country."

"This country. The U.S. of A."

"Right."

Breedlove narrowed his eyes. "How old are you?"

"Forty-eight."

The detective nodded. "Look a lot younger."

"Clean living."

Breedlove sat back, studied him for a moment. "You always got a smart-ass answer for everything, Mr. Fallon?"

"No," said Fallon, and smiled.

Breedlove sighed. He glanced down at the notebook again, looked up. "You're not married."

"No."

"Divorced?"

"Yes."

Breedlove raised his pen. "Name and address?"

"I don't think so."

He looked up. "Pardon?" He wasn't smiling.

"I said I don't think so."

The detective's face shuttered down. Eyebrows lowered, mouth grim, he said, "Why is that?"

"Three reasons," Fallon said. "First, I haven't seen her for nearly twenty years. She and I aren't the same people now. She doesn't deserve to be bothered with all this stuff. Second, she lives in Greece, so you're going to have a hard time talking to her. Third, even if you do talk to her, you won't understand a thing she says, because she speaks only Greek. Sorry."

"So you think that maybe you won't be giving me her name and address."

"No," said Fallon. "I don't think it anymore. I'm not going to give you her name and address."

"Listen," said Breedlove, leaning forward. His voice had a rasp to it that hadn't been there before. He thumbed a button on his recorder, then rested his elbows on his thighs and put his hands together, fingers locked. His eyes narrowing, he looked across the table at Fallon. "How about this, Mr. Fallon. How about I take you downtown and throw your clever ass into some crappy damn cell for three or four days and we put some serious pressure on you. I mean some very *serious* goddamn pressure. Are you ready for that?"

"You bet," said Fallon. He set his mug on the coffee table and stood, shoving his hands into his pockets. "Let's go. On our way downtown, can we turn on the siren?"

Breedlove sighed again. "Sit down, Mr. Fallon."

"I'm curious to see what a judge says about all this. Elderly man, working at a legally recognized place of worship, is thrown in jail for not providing the address of a woman he hasn't seen in twenty years. A woman who lives ten thousand miles away." He nodded toward the recorder on the coffee table. "Isn't that why you turned off your Starfleet tricorder, Captain? So no one could hear you threaten me with that crap?"

Breedlove snorted. "Elderly man."

Fallon smiled. "More elderly than I used to be."

"Just sit down, Mr. Fallon." He sighed again—inhaled a deep

breath, blew it slowly out. "Look," he said finally. "I take my job seriously. I can't help it. And sometimes, okay, sometimes I might get a little carried away. Okay? So now would you just sit down, Mr. Fallon?"

"I'm not sure I can sit, Detective. Your apology really choked me up."

"Not an apology. An explanation. Sit down, Mr. Fallon."

"*Please.*"

Breedlove winced. "What?"

Fallon said, "Would you sit down, Mr. Fallon, *please.*"

The detective studied him for a moment, and then he sat back and laughed. "You really are a first-string asshole," he said. "You know that, right?"

Mildly, Fallon shrugged. "You're not the first to say so."

Grinning, Breedlove shook his head. He looked up at Fallon and made his face go serious again. "Would you sit down, Mr. Fallon, please?"

"Sure." Fallon took his hands from his pockets and sat down. He took a sip of tea.

Breedlove said, "Why not tell me you lost track of her? Why not say you didn't know where she was?"

"No lying allowed in the monastery. Come to Dunedin some Sunday and I'll explain how I won the Gulf War."

"I'll pass, thanks."

Fallon smiled. "You're not the first to say so."

Detectives Breedlove and Foster left at 2:00 a.m., Breedlove carrying in his jacket pocket the list of names and addresses that Fallon had given him.

Fallon and Bhante said their goodbyes from the front door. Bhante was wearing his long red cotton robe; Fallon was still wearing his gray sweatpants and sweatshirt.

When Fallon shut the door, Bhante said, "Can we talk for a minute, Phil? Finally?"

As they walked into the living room, Fallon smiled. "The MITs have all gone to bed?"

Bhante giggled. Then he scowled dramatically and waved his hand again, back and forth. "No jokes, Phil. They are monks in training. And this situation is very serious." He sat down on the big white sofa.

"That's what Detective Breedlove told me," said Fallon, and sat down several feet away on the same sofa.

Triumphantly Bhante said, "You see? You will get us into trouble." To punctuate this, he crossed his legs beneath him on the broad white cushion.

"I don't think so, Bhante," said Fallon. "Myself, maybe, but not the monastery. How was your detective?"

Bhante had finished adjusting his robe. He laid his lands on his lap. "Detective Foster. He was a very nice man, Phil. He was extremely interested in Buddhism and the monastery. He said he would be coming back at some time, so he could learn more."

"If you're thinking about holding a cushion open for him, I'd recommend you not bother."

"Not bother?"

"He probably wasn't telling you the entire truth."

Bhante blinked. "He would lie? An American policeman would lie?"

"Legally. It's written right into their precepts."

"Now you are joking again, Phil."

"No joke. By law, for policemen in this country, lying is completely permitted—which most of them think means 'actively encouraged.'"

"No, no. Not in a monastery."

"Bhante, they don't see this place as a monastery or as anything special. For them it's just a place where a bunch of weird foreigners and old hippy-dippy types hang around, staring at their navels."

Bhante frowned. "I have heard of this navel staring. But who is it who stares at a navel? Why would he do such a thing?"

"It's not just any navel. It's his own navel."

"Yes yes." Impatiently.

"Or *her* own navel." He smiled. "Sorry, Bhante, but you've really got to mention the women."

"Yes yes, you keep saying. I know that. But, Phil, who does this staring business?"

"No one. Thinking that anyone does that, Bhante, is just ignorance. There's a lot of ignorance going around."

"One of the three *kleshas*, the three unwholesome roots. Your detective—what was his name?"

"Breedlove."

"He was okay?"

"He was okay, yeah. A bit rude and controlling. He was tough. But a lot of cops get that way. They deal with horrible people sometimes, real monsters, scum of the earth, and they need to have a sense of control."

"Out of fear."

"Sure. There's a lot of that going around, too. But as a cop, I think he's pretty good. Shrewd, careful, quick on his feet."

"Shrewd?"

"Very smart."

"Very smart in what way?"

Fallon smiled. "Very smart about being smarter than other smart people. The way you are, Bhante."

Bhante giggled, then waved his hand some more. "No no no," he said. "I am a simple monk, trying to survive in a complicated world."

Fallon smiled. "And doing it fairly well."

Bhante smiled back, pleased, and then, almost exactly as Breedlove had done earlier, he made his face go serious. "But tell me, Phil. How was he shrewd?"

Fallon smiled. "He never pointed out the one obvious thing about the garage door."

Bhante sat there. At last he said, "That is okay, Phil. I can wait. I know how much you like this game."

Fallon laughed.

Bhante winced. "Shhh shhh shhh," he said, holding up a hand. "The monks." He pointed to the upstairs. He leaned forward. "What is the obvious thing?"

"The whole idea is to make us think that Mr. Jayacody got killed by accident. Right?"

Bhante said, "I suppose so."

Fallon smiled. "See? That's shrewd. You're covering your bets."

"This means what?"

"Let's deal with it later, okay? The important thing is that it never could've happened that way."

"How do you mean?"

"No garage door is going to kill anybody."

"But an accident…"

"When the door comes down, it doesn't move fast enough to kill

71

a person."

"But if he gets hit in the head?"

"It won't hit him that hard, because it *is* moving slowly. After he's been hit, he's got plenty of time to duck away. And let's say some impossible thing did happen—let's say the guy is totally deaf and the door surprised him so much that his heart stopped beating. Thing is, the guy would never have fallen the way he did, flat on his back with his throat right across the metal strip where the bottom of the door meets the floor."

"But—"

"Excuse me, Bhante, but let me finish. Please. You can 'but' me later."

Bhante giggled. Lightly, he flapped his fingers in the air at Fallon, once, twice. "Go go go."

"So when I left the garage, before the sitting meditation, the garage door was down. When I found Mr. Jayacody after the walking meditation, the door was down again. Before he got trapped underneath it, he—or someone else—had opened it. How?"

"That's what *I'm* asking *you*, Phil," he said, and sat back, satisfied.

Fallon smiled, then explained about the two remote controls being unavailable, one in his jacket, one in the locked Toyota. "Let's say," he continued, "for the sake of argument, that the bad guy somehow has a matching remote. From some other garage door. And it works on ours."

"Is that possible?"

Fallon smiled. "Remotely," he said.

Bhante laughed. Then he clapped his hand over his mouth and shot a glance toward the upstairs. He pulled his hand away and raised his forefinger, like a professor. He grinned. "But possible."

"Anything is possible, Bhante. But many things are unlikely. How would he know it matched? Wouldn't he have needed—"

"—needed to try it before he came."

"Exactly. But how would he do that? There's someone in the house all day long. People bringing you food, people bringing you questions. All day long, people in and out. And a lot of the time, I'm in the garage, working on something. No one can see me in there because there aren't any windows. But I'm in there, off and on, all day long, and everyone knows it. The bad guy would probably be spotted."

Bhante nodded. "Perhaps, yes. Let us simply say *perhaps* for now. But you said *first*. What is second?"

"There are sensors that help control the door's movement. They're another reason that the whole story is hooey. If anyone steps into the open driveway while the door is going down, the sensors tell the door to stop moving."

"Infrared, yes?" Bhante very much liked gadgets, and he knew quite a lot about them.

"Yes. When I got out there, after the meeting was over, I saw that someone had moved the sensors—apparently to make the door stop three inches higher."

"Hah!" said Bhante. "Suicide!"

"No. Sorry."

"Ah."

Fallon explained to Bhante what he had explained to Detective Breedlove. The door, the overhead light, the likelihood of the murderer coming into the house through the second back door.

"No no, Phil," said Bhante. "It could not have been one of us, one of the members."

"Bhante, we'll get to that in a minute."

"We have not got to 'covering my bet.' Do you remember that?"

"Perfectly. We'll get to it."

"And we have not got to what Detective Lovebreed *did not say about the garage door.*"

Fallon smiled. "Breedlove."

Bhante waved his hand dismissively. "Whatever."

"You know," said Fallon, still smiling, "if this were a mystery story, or a book or a movie, you'd be the one figuring it all out."

Bhante raised his eyebrows and pointed his forefinger at himself. "I would?"

Fallon said, "There are mystery-solving holy men, religious sleuths, all over the place. There are Catholic priests, Catholic nuns, medieval monks, Jewish rabbis. Why not a Theravada monk?"

"Sleuths?"

"Private detectives. Like Sherlock Holmes."

"Yes yes, with his famous Doctor Watson. But why are you not telling me, Phil, *what it is that Detective Breedlove is not saying about the garage door?* You said it was *obvious.*"

"It is. The whole plan, everything about it, is totally stupid. It's so stupid that it's crazy. Moving the sensors and not moving them back. Physically putting the body where it couldn't possibly have fallen on its own. Trying to make it look like he was killed by a rogue garage door."

Bhante was frowning. "Rogue?"

"Lunatic," said Fallon. "A lunatic garage door. None of that could ever happen. And Breedlove never mentioned how impossible it was."

"Perhaps he does not agree with your theory, Phil."

"Bhante, trust me. He agrees. He's a cop, and he also knows all about garage doors. He knows that one of the members is responsible."

"I do not accept this. No, Phil. It has to be someone else, someone from Mr. Jayacody's background. None of our people knew Mr. Jayacody."

"None of them admitted to knowing him. But there's no doubt about it, Bhante. The two of them—Mr. Jayacody and the murderer—definitely knew each other."

"And from where does this conclusion come?"

Fallon smiled. "Your English has really improved over this past year."

"Stop it, please, Phil. Where?"

"Okay. First thing. The bad guy—we'll call him Mr. X. If he's not a member, then there's no reason for him to meet with Mr. Jayacody here. They could've met anywhere else. Right?"

"Yes, of course."

"So for some reason, Mr. Jayacody felt this was a safe place for him. And so did Mr. X. But Mr. X had to know about this house and the way it worked. He had to know about the walking meditation, which would give him a chance to meet privately with Mr. Jayacody. He had to know about the second back door, which gave him a chance to get into the house and then into the garage. He had to know that he could open the electric door from in there."

"Yes but..." He paused.

"Bhante. He has to be one of us."

Looking off, Bhante sucked in a huge volume of air, and then he slowly released it in little puffs, like a steam locomotive.

When he was done, he turned to Fallon. "So now," he said sadly, "we must determine who he was, this Mr. X. person."

"We could let Breedlove and Foster figure it out."

"It is better that we know first."

"I agree. But I think I know already."

Bhante looked at him. "You know who killed Mr. Jayacody?"

"I think so, yeah."

"Who?"

"First we have to—"

"First!" said Bhante. "First first first! Everything is a first! There are never any seconds! Why are there no seconds in this world of yours, Phil?"

Silently, Fallon was laughing.

Bhante watched him for a moment and then he giggled. He shook his head. He ran his hand over his scalp. He put his elbow on his knee, opened his hand, and notched his chin into his palm. "Anger. The second of the three *kleshas*. It is a very bad thing." He sat up straight, put his hands on his knees. "So. First."

"First we make a plan," Fallon said.

"Aargh," said Bhante. "Phil, I am guessing that you have already made a plan. Am I correct?"

"Yes, Bhante. As usual, you are."

Bhante waved the flattery away. "Is it legal?"

"Not entirely."

"Then, Phil, no. I am sorry, truly, but you know I cannot permit the monastery to become involved in something illegal."

"I'm fairly certain that we can get around the illegal part. The important thing is that the plan is highly moral."

"Highly moral."

"Highly."

Another sigh from Bhante. "All right, Phil. Tell me the plan."

"Nice neighborhood," Fallon said.

"Very nice, yes," said Bhante.

The morning sun was splashing brightly all around them as Fallon sailed the Toyota Land Cruiser through Carrollwood, a well-maintained and well-fed suburb northwest of Tampa.

For the first time this morning, Bhante ran his hand over his shiny scalp. "I worry about the monks in training," he said. "I worry if they will be okay with the detectives."

"As I said, Bhante," said Fallon, "I think they'll be fine."

"Do you think the detectives will be angry we are gone?"

"They didn't ask us to be there, and we didn't tell them we would be. We had an emergency and we had to take care of it. The detectives want to talk to the monks, and they can still do that. And then they can start talking to the rest of the people on the list I gave to Breedlove. I hope that we can get all this finished before the two of them get out here."

Bhante turned to him. "Phil. Be honest, please. Do you believe this will work?"

"Bhante," he said, keeping his eyes on the road, "honestly, I don't know. But I do know it's the only thing we can do that might help." He glanced over at the monk. "*Samsara*, Bhante. Human life." He looked back at the road. "No guarantees."

"No," said Bhante. "Only change." He nodded firmly. "Onward," he said.

Fallon smiled. "I think we're nearly there."

Bhante squinted out the windshield. "Yes. Up here. The blue one."

The house was a long, handsome ranch-style home, pale blue like a tropical sky, set back on a broad well-tended lawn as green as a golf course. There were two huge live oak trees elaborately draped with Spanish moss, one at each side of the yard. Their thick dark limbs met together overhead and their leaves shaded both lawn and house. It all seemed cool and comfortable and calm.

Fallon and Bhante opened the doors of the Land Cruiser, stepped out onto the brick driveway.

Fallon asked Bhante, "Are we sure he's going to be home?"

"He is retired, Phil. He is always home."

They walked up the brick pathway to the front door. They took off their sunglasses and Bhante reached out and pressed the button on the jamb. They heard the muffled electronic chimes ring within.

Tucking his glasses into the cloth bag he always carried, Bhante smiled.

"What?" Fallon said. He hooked the left temple of his own glasses into the collar of his sweat shirt.

"The Sri Lankan National Anthem," said Bhante. He cleared his throat, then softly sang, "*Sri Lanka matha—*"

The door opened and Shehara, Mrs. Gunarante, stood there smiling happily up at them, wearing a long gray skirt and a white silk blouse. In her mid-fifties, she was a small vivid woman with a flurry of beautiful black hair, artfully tied back now, and with precise, delicate features and a precise, delicate shape. Watching them with large brown eyes, she gave Bhante and Fallon a graceful *namaste* bow, her small elegant hands pressed elegantly together. "Bhante," she said. "And Phil. How *wonderful*. Welcome to our house."

"Thank you, Shehara," said Bhante, returning the bow. "We—"

"Ah, Bhante!" said a deep, expansive voice, and then Thari, Mr. Gunarante, suddenly appeared behind and above his wife, big and broad-shouldered and white-haired. "And Phil!" He gave Bhante a bow, and threw out his big hand to Fallon, who offered his own hand and let Thari's hand crunch at it.

"Come in, come in," Thari boomed. He turned to his wife. "My darling, could we do a lovely pot of that new tea?"

She laughed. "We?"

Bhante said, "Oh no no no. Please, Shehara, do not bother."

"Bhante," she said, "it's no bother, the water is on the stove. You go with Thari, and I'll join you all in a minute."

"Thank you, thank you," Bhante said to her, then turned to her husband and said, "Thari, Phil and I were driving nearby and I wanted Phil to see your lake."

Thari glanced at his watch. "Perfect timing!" he exclaimed. He grinned at Bhante and Fallon. "My best friend is arriving any moment now."

Bhante and Fallon had taken off their sandals and set them with the other sandals and sneakers lined up beside the front door. Bhante smiled politely at Thari. "Your best friend?"

"Come, come, I'll show you."

They followed him. He wore a light blue tattersall linen shirt, its tails hanging loose, its sleeves rolled carefully back, and a pair of gray twill trousers. Fallon noticed that there was an irregular lump beneath the shirt, just at the back of Thari's right hip.

The living room through which they walked was spare and simple, the furniture low and made of bent oak and sleek off-white leather. The only indication that a Buddhist family lived here was a graceful oak table, to the left of the fireplace, that supported a small but very good copy of a famous Gandhara seated Buddha statue. In front of the statue was a simple silver candle holder that held an unlighted tea candle; a small oblong wooden incense box, intricately carved; and a slim silver vase that held a single red rose.

On the thick white pile of the carpet beneath, side by side, were two plump meditation cushions.

The interior was all one huge open space, and at the far side, beyond a low divider that supported the stereo system and the large flat digital television, was the dining area. Someone had turned around a couple of the chairs by the huge triple windows so they looked out on the shimmering bright blue lake.

"There he is!" said Thari. "Look!" He pointed toward the right. "You see him?"

"Yes!" said Bhante. "Thari—my goodness! What *is* that thing?"

Thari said something in Sinhala that Fallon didn't understand. Then the man turned to Fallon. "Phil!" he said, "I just went dry on the English. What are they called?"

"Otters," Fallon said. "River otters."

"He's coming here!" Bhante said. "To this house!" He clapped his hands together, delighted.

"It's completely *verboten*, of course," said Thari, "but someone insists on putting bits of trash fish out along the shore there. You see it?"

Fallon said, "That trash fish looks a lot like fillet of brook trout. From the supermarket."

First Breedlove, then Bhante, and now Thari. Like the others, he made his face go serious. "Sounds like women's work to me." He laughed a big booming laugh. He looked to his right and said, "Hah. Speak of the devil."

Shehara had returned, carrying a large tea tray and, once again, smiling happily. She stopped, and the smile fell away. She looked at the three men, one after the other, and then her delicate shoulders sagged slightly. She began to cry.

"*My darling*," said Thari, turning his big body toward her.

She was wavering slightly, back and forth. She looked at her husband. "They know, Thari," she said. Her voice was frail and feathery.

Fallon was nearest. He sprang forward and grabbed the tray just as she began to sink. He wheeled around, clutching at it, keeping it away from her.

Her husband, too, had sprung forward, and he managed to catch her, scoop her up into his arms, before she collapsed to the floor.

* * *

"How did you know, Phil?" Thari asked him.

They were all sitting at the dining table, Thari and Shehara on one side, Bhante and Fallon on the other, from where they had a full view of the lake. Thari had arranged the tea settings, Fallon had poured the tea. The otter was gone.

"Thari," said Fallon. "You're a Sri Lankan army officer who was seconded to the British Army. You're a sophisticated man. And a worldly man. You know about lots of things, including garage door openers." He smiled. "You were the last person anyone would suspect."

Thari nodded. "I oversold it."

"A tad."

"The sensors?"

"That was part of it, yeah. All you needed were the high and low adjusters on the control box, but you wanted to look inept. And I realized that you must have kept an extra remote for the garage when you bought the opener for us. With the extra remote, it would only take you a few minutes to arrange the door opener. Time was important. You didn't have much of it."

"You knew all along?"

"I wasn't positive. One thing I'm curious about."

"Yes?"

"I don't think you used the ladder to get to the box."

Thari shook his head. "No. I climbed up onto the hood of the Land Cruiser."

Fallon smiled. "You're very agile, Thari."

Thari smiled back. "For an old man," he said. "This morning I burned my jeans and my sneakers in the barbecue pit outside. And the gloves, too, of course."

Shehara put her left hand atop her husband's right. "I told you Phil was clever."

"You were spot on," he told her. "You always are, my sweet. I hate you."

Smiling, she gently turned his hand on the table, and then put out her right, so she could cradle his between both of hers. "I know you do, darling."

Fallon said, "What did Jayacody have on you?"

"My daughter," said Thari. "And my grandchildren. They were in Sri Lanka. He told me that he could have all of them killed in an instant. A snap of the finger. It would take merely a phone call."

"What was he selling? Drugs? Women?"

"Women."

"He was a vile, filthy swine," said Shehara.

Thari looked down at her, squeezed her hand, turned back to Fallon. "He began during the war. The civil war in Sri Lanka. You know about this, Phil?"

"Some."

"Like all wars, it was a horror. They committed crimes, the Tamil Tigers. The enemy. But so did we. The Sri Lankan Army. I was not involved—I was with the British then. But had I been there, probably I would have committed crimes as well."

"You do not know this," said Bhante.

"Know it, no. Fear it, yes." He looked at Fallon. "Jayacody did commit crimes. He was responsible for a great many of the Tamils who disappeared. This was well known among the upper echelons of the Army."

Fallon interrupted. "The other Sri Lankans here. They didn't know about him?"

"No. No civilians did. But even when he was busy with those evils, he was committing others. Kidnapping young Tamil girls, some of them only twelve or thirteen years old, orphans—orphans that he himself had *made* orphans—selling them to traffickers who carried them on cargo ships, in container boxes, to England and the States. His business grew and he finally established his own trafficking systems and routes, leased his own cargo ships."

"Greed," said Bhante. He looked at Phil. "The third *klesha*."

"He knows all the *kleshas* intimately, Bhante," said Thari. "Now he deals with young girls from Myanmar. He has army connections there, of course."

"How did you learn all this?" Fallon asked.

"Last week, after he contacted me, I called some friends in Sri Lanka and India. I still have my own contacts in the Army. And elsewhere."

"Cell phone?"

"Satellite phone. The GPS function was shut off."

"So the location is blind. No one will know it. And the line is encrypted?"

"Yes, of course. Not the standard encryption, the Chinese can crack that now. But some new software created by Mossad. How do you know about such things, Phil?"

"I read a lot," Fallon said. "You're very well prepared, Thari."

"Boys and their toys," said Shehara, smiling sadly as she rubbed her husband's forearm.

He gazed down on her. "I have to say, I'm very thankful for them."

"Oh I am, too, darling. I am. But sometimes..." She smiled again, sadly. "There was another world once. You remember it?"

He nodded. "Always."

Bhante said, "With the GPS off and the Israeli encryption, your conversations are safe?"

"For now," Thari said. "In another month, who knows?"

"Okay," said Fallon. "What did he want from you?"

"Bookkeeping, basically. He has people here in Tampa, off-loading the 'merchandise' at the port. They dispose of the girls through various intermediaries, and the intermediaries pay off his people. My new job, according to Jayacody, was to get encrypted email reports of each transaction, from his people and from the intermediaries, and verify that the money—his money—had been put into particular Caribbean accounts, and then give him all the records on a USB thumb drive when I met with him here."

Fallon said, "No verifiable contact between any of the accounts and himself."

"Exactly."

"Paranoid."

"Evil people suckle their paranoia, Phil. It's one of the things that keeps them alive."

"Why did he pick you?"

"I was here. I spoke English and Sinhala. I was subject to leverage because of my family. And I think he may have heard what I said about him when I retired. I think he welcomed an opportunity to put me in my place. Put me in a hopeless position, a position that further empowered his own."

"The pig," said Shehara.

Fallon nodded. "Okay. So what was your plan?"

"Last night, at 1930 hours here—" he turned to Bhante, "—while we were still listening to you, Bhante—it was 0500 hours in Sri Lanka. A detachment of men covertly entered a house in the capital, Columbo, exfiltrated my daughter—" He turned to Bhante again, said something in Sinhala, then turned back to Fallon, "—exfiltrated my daughter and her children. They left a small contingent there in the house, to deal with anyone who might come looking, and they drove my family to a private plane that would fly them to England."

"Did anyone come looking?"

"About five hours later. A small squad of former Special Forces. They seem to have disappeared afterward."

"On their own?" Fallon asked.

"We helped them."

"The house in England?"

"Provided by a friend of a friend. Safe. We've spoken to our daughter."

"You're planning to join her. You and Shehara."

"We're waiting to see if this dies down."

"If it doesn't?"

"I will surrender."

"And I," said Shehara.

He smiled at her. "She did nothing."

She sat upright, looking straight at Fallon. "I approved," she said.

Fallon said to Thari, "You know you're both in danger."

"Of course," said Thari. "But friends are close. Here in Tampa. And I have resources of my own."

"I noticed. That's a Browning Hi-Power you're carrying?"

Thari frowned. "Yes. The DBA version. Double action."

"A good weapon. Fourteen rounds, nine millimeters."

"Phil, you're not merely clever. You're a devil."

"I read a lot. You know any American spooks? CIA, NSA?"

"A few."

"Will they back you?"

"Help me in some way?"

"Right."

"Some might. One for certain."

"CIA?

"NSA."

"You've kept duplicates of all the records you delivered to Jayacody?"

"Of course. In the cloud—I believe that he and his people have hacked my computer. For the cloud I use one in the public library, less than a mile away. Everything first decrypted and then encrypted again with my own software. Done on a second computer, one with no wi-fi access."

"Good."

Bhante said, "Phil has a plan."

Fallon said to Thari, "Call your friend at the NSA. Tell him the situation. Tell him we're going to be dickering with the Tampa cops. Ask him what he can do."

"You think I should do this now?"

Fallon smiled. "I think you should've done it yesterday. But *now* is what we've got. And when you're done with him, call the others— so long as you trust them—and ask what they can do."

"I don't like to bother my friends."

"You've already bothered some."

"My daughter was involved."

"Bother a few more, Thari. Please."

Thari turned to Shehara. "My darling?"

"As I said," she smiled. "Phil is very smart."

Detectives Breedlove and Foster followed Shehara Gunarante into the house. She turned to say something but saw that they were already taking off their shoes.

"Thank you," she told them.

Detective Breedlove said, "No problem, ma'am." Detective Foster, younger and thinner, smiled like a high school kid. Mrs. Gunarante was a formidable woman.

She waited until they finished, then said, "This way, please," and led them out to the dining area, where Fallon, Bhante, and Thari Gunarante sat along the far side of the table. There were two empty chairs to the right of Thari, who sat at the end.

Thari stood. He leaned over and shook hands with both men. Fallon watched them. They both took Thari's grip well.

Thari was no longer carrying the Browning. "Please, gentlemen," he said, "have a seat." With his big hand he indicated the two chairs opposite him.

Thari was himself a formidable person. Bigger and taller than anyone else in the room, he had the stark, lined face of an American Indian chieftain who broods about the White Eyed Devils slowly but relentlessly stealing out across his prairie.

The two policemen sat down on one side of the table, and Shehara sat down next to her husband. Fallon sat down between her and Bhante.

"Okay, Mr. Fallon," said Breedlove, looking over at him. "This is your party. What have you got?"

"Thanks for coming," he said, nodding first to Breedlove and then to Foster. "As you know now, these people are Mr. and Mrs. Gunarante. Mr. Gunarante is going to tell you what happened to Mr. Jayacody, and why it happened. Then I'm going to explain a few other things."

"Terrific," said Breedlove, and he smiled at Foster. Foster smiled back, but a bit weakly now, like an embarrassed kid.

"The best thing would be," said Fallon, "that you hold off on your questions until Mr. Gunarante is finished. Okay?"

Breedlove smiled. "Fine." Foster nodded. He glanced at Shehara, glanced away.

Fallon turned to Thari. "Mr. Gunarante?"

Thari put his hands together on the table, fingers interlinked. He cleared his throat. "I killed Kosala Jayacody," he began.

He detailed who Mr. Jayacody had been during the Sri Lankan Civil War and after it—murderer, kidnapper, human trafficker. He detailed how Jayacody had extorted Mr. Gunarante's assistance by threatening the lives of his daughter and grandchildren. He detailed how he had gotten his daughter to safety, although he failed to mention the various paramilitary factions that were in and out of the Columbo house that morning.

Finally, finished with his tale, he sat back in his chair and crossed his arms over his chest. Shehara, beside him, did exactly the same.

Breedlove asked Fallon, "So can I talk now, Mr. Fallon? Is that all right with you?"

Fallon smiled. "Go right ahead, Detective."

Breedlove turned to Thari. "Mr. um..."

"Gunarante," said Fallon.

"Gunarante," said Breedlove. "Mr. Gunarante, that's a great story. It's definitely a great story. But, see, there's no actual proof of any of it, and as policemen we need to have something that at least *looks* like proof. You follow me?" He turned to Fallon. "I don't see any proof here."

"That's where I come in, Detective," said Fallon.

"Right," said Breedlove. "Then come on in, Mr. Fallon."

"First of all," said Fallon, "We have an affidavit signed by a highly placed figure within the U.S. National Security Agency verifying that the information Mr. Gunarante has provided to you about Mr. Jayacody is all true. We have other affidavits from people within the Central Intelligence Agency substantiating the same thing."

"Where are these affidavits?"

"They've all been sent to Mr. Gunarante's attorney, who's already waiting for you down at police headquarters."

"An attorney?"

"Robert P. Rosenthal."

"He's got Rosenthal? Wait a minute. Rosenthal retired."

"Yes, he did, but he's an old friend of Mr. Gunarante's."

Rosenthal had agreed to help, even though the lawyer, after listening to Fallon's plan, believed that the thing would never come to trial.

Breedlove caught himself taking a deep breath. He puffed it out in a kind of cough, cleared his throat, and then looked out across the lake.

"There's one other thing, Detective," said Fallon.

Breedlove looked at him, his face weary. "Yeah?"

"Those records? The ones that Mr. Gunarante got from Jayacody's people and handed over to Jayacody?"

Shifting ever so slightly in his seat, Breedlove raised an eyebrow. "Yeah?"

"Before he handed them over, Mr. Gunarante copied them all, decrypted them, and slapped them into the cloud. You know about the cloud, right, Detective?"

Harshly: "Yeah I know about the god—" he swallowed, glanced at Mrs. Gunarante, cleared his throat again, nodded, "—I know about the cloud."

"Right. So what he's got are the account numbers and email addresses of a lot of people involved in human trafficking. Right here in Tampa. Right now."

Fallon sipped tea from the fragile white cup that Shehara had brought from the kitchen. "This is something," he said, "that the FBI would like to know, and the taxation people would like to know, both here and in Sri Lanka. The police and the army in Sri Lanka would also probably like to know it."

For a moment, Breedlove stared off across the lake. Sunlight still glinted and shivered along the water.

He turned to Fallon. "This could be a pretty big deal."

"That occurred to me."

Bhante wanted to go down to the police station with the Gunarantes, but Thari insisted that he and Shehara would be fine, and he told Bhante that it would be much better for Bhante to get back to the monastery and help other people. Shehara agreed, and so did Detective Breedlove, who said that Thari would probably be home again within a few hours. Thari shook Fallon's hand again, but with a warm smile and far less hydraulic pressure. And Shehara put her hands on his shoulders, pulled him gently down toward herself, and kissed him softly on the cheek. She smelled faintly of night-blooming jasmine.

Then they all trekked outside to arrange themselves in the car, along with Bhante, to say goodbye. Only Fallon and Breedlove lingered, standing in the living room, looking out at the flash and dance of sunlight along the lake.

Breedlove spoke. "You never told me you were a cop."

Fallon turned to him, smiled. "You never asked. It was a long time ago."

"A famous cop, too. Just like Frank Serpico."

Fallon shook his head. "I was taller."

"But you were a whistleblower, just like him. Not in New York. A smaller place. Portland."

"You checked me out."

"I always check out a wise ass. You testified against other cops. Corruption."

"That's right."

"They retired you, even though you'd only been there a few years."

"I got shot."

"By another cop."

Fallon nodded. "Friendly fire."

"You got a full pension. Medical."

"They wanted me out of there. Bad for the troops. Especially if I got shot again."

"You know what I don't like?"

"What's that?"

"Cops who testify against other cops."

"I can understand that."

"You know what I don't like even more than cops who testify against other cops?"

"No idea."

"Cops who shoot other cops."

Fallon smiled again. "I have similar feelings."

Detective Breedlove put out his hand. "You did some good here. Thanks."

Fallon shook it. "Thanks. So did you."

"Phil?" said Bhante as they were driving through Carrollwood, on their way back to the monastery.

"Yes, Bhante."

"When you were telling me about the remote controls for the garage opener, you already knew about the extra one that Thari had."

"I told you last night. I guessed. I wasn't sure."

"And the adjustment of those switches in the control box?"

"Again, a guess. I wasn't sure about those, either. But someone had to fiddle with them. Probably someone familiar with that particular opener. Like Thari."

"But you didn't tell your detective about the guesses."

"My loyalty isn't to the cops, Bhante. And I never lied to him."

"And you never told him the entire truth."

"Bhante, we talked about this last night. I didn't know the entire truth. I was only guessing."

Bhante nodded. "Guessing, yes." For a few moments he watched the houses skim swiftly by. Then, still watching them, he said, "Detective Breedlove was not the only person who did not receive the entire truth."

Fallon looked over at him and smiled. "No. As you pointed out this morning, you didn't receive it for a while yourself. You pointed that out last night, too."

"But why the delay?"

"I wanted to see how persuasively I could keep the focus from falling on Thari. At least until we talked to him ourselves. And I did tell you. Right there in the living room last night. You knew everything long before Breedlove did."

Bhante continued to stare out the window. After quite a long time, he inhaled deeply and then exhaled. "Yes. That is true. And we were able, the two of us, to correct the situation and keep Thari and Shehara safe."

"That's right."

Bhante ran his hand along his skull. "We did well, Phil."

Fallon smiled. "We certainly did." He looked at Bhante, saw that he was smiling too.

Bhante looked out the window and watched the houses for a while.

A few minutes later, he said, "Phil, you write, do you not?"

"Write?" said Fallon. "What do you mean?"

Bhante turned to him. "I see you at the computer, tap-tap-tapping."

"Email. And monastery accounts. I don't really write anything."

"Hmm."

Bhante looked out the window for a few more moments. Then he turned again to Fallon. "What about Mr. Conlan?"

"The older man?"

"Not that old," insisted Bhante.

"In his sixties somewhere. He's retired."

"Yes, but he was once a writer."

"He was, yes."

"He wrote books."

"Yes."

"What kind of books?"

"Advanced comic books, he calls them."

"He is being clever, yes?"

"Yes."

"What does he mean?"

"I think he means thrillers, maybe a mystery or two."

"Like Sherlock Holmes?"

"Probably not as lucrative."

"Lucrative means financially successful."

"It does."

"Do you think he would be interested in writing a story—"

Fallon smiled. "Bhante, I know where you're going with this."

Bhante returned the smile. "Where?"

"Would Mr. Conlan be interested in writing a story about a

monk like you who solved crimes?'

"Not exactly like me, of course. But he would be smart and clever. Shrewd, yes? And, Phil, he would have an assistant, a steward, like yourself, who was very shrewd also."

"A sidekick."

"Yes, a sidekick like Dr. Watson. And there would be many interesting people as members of the monastery, writers and painters, funny people and clever people. The readers, they could learn interesting true facts about Buddha and Buddhism! It might help people to become enlightened! Phil, what do you think?"

"What do I think about a story with you as the brilliant sleuth and me as your faithful sidekick, a story that would help people with their Buddha studies and maybe get them enlightened?"

"Yes!"

Fallon laughed. "Bhante," he said, "I think it would be wonderful."

This issue is a good one for finding writers with strong resumés with their novels as well as short stories. It really is a difficult thing to do but Sylvia Warsh's novels have not only been tagged with a number of award nominations, the second book in her Dr. Rebecca Temple series, Find Me Again, *took home an Edgar award for Best Paperback Original. More recently, her short story "The Cabin in the Woods" was nominated for a Derringer Award in the best short story category. With this story, Sylvia brings us a twisty tale from the world of fine art. And murder, of course.*

The Veiled Heart
Sylvia Maultash Warsh

Henry sat with the receiver to his ear, wishing he hadn't picked up the phone. It was after hours; he could've let it go to message. While the man's voice harangued him, he searched the wall of familiar lithographs for escape, landing on Dalí's sundial. Yellow and dreamlike, the disk contained Dalí's right eye staring into the inscrutable distance, a curl of his famous moustache.

Henry was in the business of making sense of things, but he had failed badly this time. "I understand you're upset—" he began.

"Don't try using your shrink tricks on me," the man shot back. "I'm not upset! I'm mad as hell! If you'd been paying attention, my wife would still be alive."

Henry took in a sharp breath. "You have no call to say that, Mr. Richmond. She never gave any indication—she never talked about... taking her life. It was a shock to me too."

"Then what kind of a shrink are you, Dr. Lester? All those years she spent going to therapy and you couldn't figure her out. You were supposed to help her. You should've seen it coming."

Angela Richmond had saved up all the antidepressants Henry had ever prescribed for her, then used them to commit suicide.

"And those creepy pictures in your office. Crazy people don't

90

need to see that shit."

What a lout, thought Henry. He glanced up at the lithograph Angela had liked: a woman's shoulders with a bouquet of flowers where the head should be.

"They're part of the therapeutic process," he said. Almost true.

He liked to ask his patients what they saw in the various Dalí lithographs that hung in the office. Angela had gazed at the piece with the flowering head and said she wished it were her. She complained her husband kept to himself and made her feel alone. She said she didn't know him. Henry wasn't about to throw that in the man's face since it was confidential. It turned out she was just as unknowable. He tried not to blame himself. Her death had unnerved him. An elegant woman in her late fifties, she was deeply unhappy, her grown children having moved away. She was his second suicide in over twenty-five years of practice. Did anyone really know the people around them, even those close?

Henry's father, for example, moody after a recent heart attack, had surprised him with an ultimatum. Take over the family company or be disinherited. He should've expected it; his father had regularly dismissed Henry's medical career, the patients who depended on him. A psychiatrist wasn't a *real* doctor, all he did was talk. Why couldn't he be a surgeon? Now *that* was a doctor. The old man had always been unreasonable—that was how he had amassed a fortune. Though he had started small, building a few houses in Toronto after the war, decades of risk-taking and non-stop work had helped Stanley Lester build the business into a real estate empire. Henry depended on revenue coming from his place on the board of Lester Holdings. He couldn't afford to buy Salvador Dalí art on what psychiatrists earned from the Ontario Health Insurance Plan. And without Dalí, life would've been inexplicable. The artist interpreted existence for him. The flat shadowy landscapes, the headless images that could have emerged from his dreams made him understand the world better. Not the way it appeared, but as it really *was*: chaotic, absurd, cruel.

Why couldn't his sister Suzy take over the company? She was the older sibling and had helped run the business for years. Even if her methods weren't always on the up-and-up. She was known to bid low on a contract, and once successful, would encounter "setbacks" that inflated prices. Their father thought this behavior offensive in a woman, though he would have deemed it business acumen in Henry.

She was too much of a man, their father said, no wonder her personal life was a mess—two ex-husbands, no children. (Henry, divorced and childless, was no better.) However, even Stan Lester had to admit the company was thriving. Suzy was a good caretaker but his father was old-school and would never leave the company in the hands of a woman.

Henry heard a tentative knock at the front door. His office was closed for the day. He lived upstairs in the old Victorian house but hadn't been expecting anyone. When he opened the door, a small wiry man in his thirties stood on the porch. His weathered skin along with the jeans and windbreaker made Henry wonder if he was about to be asked for money.

"Begging your pardon, but are you Dr. Henry Lester?"

Henry nodded.

The man cleared his throat. "My name is Ron Osmond. I have been authorized to offer you a painting that rarely comes up for sale. For your collection."

He recited this as if from memory, unused to multisyllabic words. How did the man know about his collection? Maybe one of his patients had told him.

"Who authorized you?"

"My client wishes to remain anonymous."

"I don't buy art from strangers. Tell whoever sent you I only work with legitimate agents."

"My client has had, um, financial setbacks. He wishes to keep a low profile. It's a very reasonable offer." Then, as if just remembering, he pulled a photo from his jeans' pocket.

Henry gasped.

"It's called—"

"I know what it's called, man!"

Henry took the photo from the man's hand. *The Veiled Heart!* Dalí's famous but elusive painting, long rumored to be owned by an unnamed private collector. Could this even be possible? He gaped at the photo: a gold silk cloak had been thrown over two figures crouching upon an ostensible heart, identified only by the blood-red lobe visible bottom left. The shapes outlined by the cloak appeared to be in some kind of turmoil, a long feminine torso embracing, the male other, aloof, pitiless. They threw a black shadow against the yellow-blue sky behind them, out of reach. Excruciating beauty.

He tried to calm himself. "How do I know you've got the real thing?"

"See for yourself. Come on to my place. Right now if you want."

He handed Henry a business card that he could have printed at home. Only his name, address and phone number, and strangely, in the upper corner, the profile of a horse.

"What are they asking?"

"One million. Twenty percent deposit."

Henry blinked, trying to hide his excitement. It was worth so much more. He had enough in a savings account for the deposit. He would have to sell a few investments, but that was a fleeting thought. That he might own *The Veiled Heart*! In his wildest dreams he never imagined such a thing could be possible.

"I want to see documents proving he's the legal owner. I don't buy stolen art."

"Sure. You got a car?"

Henry was wary but led the man to his Audi parked on the street. Osmond directed him south on Dufferin Street, and further west to a dreary neighbourhood lined with tired postwar apartment buildings.

A large woman with a grey ponytail watched from a second-floor balcony as Henry followed Osmond into the building. He unlocked the entrance door and led Henry down the poorly lit first floor hallway to his flat. The small dingy living room had been painted beige in some other decade.

A slim leather briefcase lay on the melamine coffee table in front of an ancient sofa. Henry declined the offer of a drink.

"May I see the painting?" he asked.

Osmond picked up the briefcase. He brought out a small oil on canvas stretched over a frame. Henry caught his breath. He took the painting reverently, wonder-struck to be holding it in his own hands. The exquisite turmoil of the cloaked figures caught at his chest. He held the painting without speaking for several minutes, his heart full. Eventually, he lifted it up to the light to examine the signature in the bottom right hand corner. Painted in yellow on the shadowy background: *Gala Salvador Dalí 1932*. The writing hand was very like the signatures on the artwork he had at home.

"Provenance?"

Osmond pulled a sheet of paper from the briefcase. "Here's a photocopy of the last bill of sale."

Henry stared at it.

> *The Veiled Heart*, oil on canvas, 24 cm. by 16 cm. was sold by XXXX in Paris to XXXX in New York on August 14, 1993 for the sum of one million dollars.

The names had been struck out with black marker.

"This tells me nothing," Henry said.

"The owner wants to remain—"

"Anonymous. You told me."

Henry didn't trust the man or the document, but he *wanted* the painting. "I'll get someone from the art gallery to take a look at it."

Osmond sat down on the edge of a captain's chair opposite the sofa. "Oh."

"You wouldn't expect me to hand over a million dollars just like that."

Osmond cleared his throat. "Of course."

"Bring it to the AGO tomorrow," he said.

"The AGO?"

"The Art Gallery of Ontario." How could this man be a go-between for art? "I'll call you to arrange a time."

The man asked for Henry's business card, in case he had to "get in touch."

Henry had a contact at the art gallery, Gilbert, who had helped him authenticate other Dalí pieces he'd bought. Part of the acquisitions staff, Gilbert had agreed at once to examine the painting, which hadn't been seen in public for years. Osmond was to bring it to Gilbert's office at 4 p.m. It was a Saturday, so Henry easily cleared his schedule.

Henry arrived early to the meeting. Gilbert, middle-aged, foppish in a yellow bow tie, had located a photograph of the painting in an old catalogue from a long-ago exhibit. Henry gazed at the blood-red lobe, the cloaked figures crouching on the heart, hidden from the viewer, hidden from each other. That's what people did—hid what they really felt, what they really wanted. All the years he'd spent exploring people's minds trying to understand. But people kept secrets, like Angela, who must have been planning her suicide all along, even as she came to her appointment week after week, never revealing what was really in her heart.

Osmond was late. Embarrassed, Henry tried the number on the business card. There was no answer. After a while, he apologized to Gilbert and left the gallery.

Two days went by. At eight in the evening, Osmond called. No apology. "You still want that painting?"

Henry's heart leaped. There was still a chance. "Why didn't you come…?"

"Can't talk. Come to my place tonight. Ten o'clock." He hung up.

The street looked different in the dark, the hulks of buildings squatting in shadow. Promptly at ten, Henry rang the bell in Osmond's lobby. He waited but no one buzzed him in. He pushed the button again, and then again. Only silence. He looked past the glass door into the lit hallway. Empty. He was thinking it time to turn around and go home, when his chest tightened, making it hard to breathe: what if he never saw *The Veiled Heart* again? Osmond must have asked him over for something other than just to play with him.

He pushed a few of the other buttons, hoping someone would unlock the door. One voice answered.

"It's me," Henry said with no remorse.

The buzzer sounded, unlocking the entrance. The fluorescent light turned the deserted entryway blue-cold. He stepped down the hall and knocked at Osmond's door. Still no answer. He put his ear to the wood. Silence. He tried the handle, sure it would be locked. To his surprise, it turned in his hand. He pushed the door open slightly.

"Osmond? You here?"

He slid the door open a few more inches. "Osmond?" The apartment was silent. Faint light emanated from the galley kitchen on the right.

With some misgivings, Henry stuck his head inside the door. The living room was dark with shadow, but he could see the coffee table and lamp had been knocked over. He moved his hand along the wall until he found the light switch.

Osmond was slumped in the captain's chair, head flopped sideways, a knife stuck in his chest. Into the heart. Henry's pulse throbbed in his ears.

He bent his ear to the man's nose. He placed two fingers over the carotid artery. No pulse, though the body was still warm. He must have died within the past hour. He looked very young, with his hair mussed.

Henry was about to call 9-1-1 on his cell, but something niggled at him about the weapon. It wasn't a knife. It was a scalpel, with only the handle visible. Not just any scalpel. An old one, like the kind he had used in his anatomy class in med school. He backed away from the body, his hands shaking. That was a weird coincidence, he thought. He had kept his old scalpel along with a few other instruments in a small case in his night table for sentimental reasons.

Something caught his eye on the floor beside the sofa. He bent over for a better look. The shock made him cry out: *The Veiled Heart* slashed open across the front! Ruined! Who would do such an obscene thing? The destruction wrenched his heart.

He had the presence of mind to avoid touching things, not to leave fingerprints, while looking for his business card, but it was nowhere to be found.

Police sirens wailed in the night, halting Henry in his tracks. When they stopped nearby, he panicked.

As neighbors' voices rose in the hall, he fled into the bedroom toward the window. He threw up the sash as far as it would go, punched out the screen, and scrambled outside into a yard, thankful the apartment was on the first floor. He crept along the side of the building. Two police cars sat in front, lights flashing. Who had called them?

The officers were busy getting inside the building when Henry skulked down the street to his car and drove off.

On his way home, he went over everything he could remember about Osmond, from the moment he had appeared at his house to the moment Henry had found the body. The police would not be able to connect him to Osmond. If he couldn't find his business card, odds were they wouldn't be able to either. Though he had done nothing wrong, Henry didn't want to see his name, or the company's, in the news.

Early the following morning, two men wearing dark suits rang his bell.

"Dr. Henry Lester?"

He nodded, his heart thumping. How had they found him? The two held up badges, but in his fog, he had trouble taking them in. They reminded him of one of Dalí's favourite painting subjects, Don Quixote and Sancho Panza, the tall bony older cop with wispy hair, the other short, burly, dark-haired.

"We'd like to ask you some questions," Don Quixote said.

"About?"

"Ron Osmond."

His heart skipped beats. "I don't believe I know him."

Sancho Panza opened a small notebook. "You made a reservation to go riding on the afternoon of May 19th at the Horse Palace. Osmond is a groom there."

Henry remembered the horse in the corner of Osmond's card. "It must be a mistake. I haven't been on a horse in years." His father used to take him and Suzy riding when they were teenagers.

Don Quixote clasped his hands in front of him. "Do you mind if we come in?"

Henry showed them into his office. They sat down on stuffed chairs while he took his seat behind the desk.

Don Quixote said, "Osmond was found murdered yesterday. Stabbed. With a scalpel."

Henry paused, trying to look shocked. "I still don't know him."

"Then how do you explain this?" Sancho Panza brought out a plastic baggie containing Henry's business card smeared in blood.

That was why he couldn't find it—the card had been in Osmond's shirt pocket beside the stab wound.

"Maybe he was looking for a psychiatrist." What else could he say?

They watched him, coolly.

"Where were you last night?"

"Here."

"Can anyone verify that?"

He opened his mouth, but nothing came out.

"A neighbour said that two days ago Osmond got out of an expensive car driven by a well-dressed older man. What kind of car do you drive, Dr. Lester?"

"An Audi."

"White?"

Henry nodded.

Sancho Panza gave his partner an *I told you so* look.

There was no point denying everything. The neighbour would be able to identify him. "Osmond came to me two days ago, offered me a Salvador Dalí painting for my collection."

Don Quixote lifted his eyes to the art on the walls. Henry wondered if he would recognize himself in the lithograph where his silhouette rode a skinny horse, holding a spear.

"Where would someone like Osmond get a Dalí painting?"

"He said he was selling it on behalf of a client."

"The client's name?"

Henry shook his head, sorrier than they could know. "His client wanted to remain anonymous."

Sancho Panza smirked.

Don Quixote said, "Do you mind if we take a look around?" Their faces were blank, obscure.

"I have nothing to hide."

Sancho Panza stood up. Henry opened the door that led to the kitchen at the back of the house, the stairs to the second floor.

Fifteen minutes later Sancho Panza returned carrying a small leather case: Henry's old anatomy kit. His eyes widened.

The younger policeman opened the case, revealing suturing scissors, forceps, needle holder, all held in place by leather loops. One of the loops was empty.

"What's missing?" the cop asked.

Henry wracked his brain trying to remember when he'd last taken out the case. "The scalpel," he murmured. "But I haven't seen it in years."

Don Quixote fixed his eyes on him. "Dr. Lester, did you kill Ron Osmond?"

"No! He was already dead when I got there."

The cops exchanged glances. "You found the body? Why didn't you tell us that right away?"

"I knew how it would look."

"You were right. It doesn't look good."

"He called, asking me to come."

"Why?"

"He didn't say...Look, I think someone's setting me up."

The men looked at him expectantly. "And who do you think would do that?"

Henry pressed his fingers over his eyelids. Who would want to destroy his life? He thought of the angry conversation from a few days earlier. The man had been unreasonable, but would he go this far to get revenge? Who knew what was in someone's heart?

"The husband of one of my patients was very upset. Mike Richmond. His wife committed suicide and he blamed me."

Don Quixote's eyebrow rose. "And were you to blame?"

If he was trying to push him off balance, it wouldn't work. "It goes along with the territory when you work with disturbed people. Sometimes they don't see a way out."

"So you think the husband staged all this?"

"I don't know. People do strange things when they're desperate."

Both cops stood up. "You'll have to come down to the station."

The detectives took Henry's fingerprints and made him wait in an interview room before questioning him again. It turned out that an expert at the AGO—Gilbert, Henry presumed—examined *The Veiled Heart* and pronounced it an excellent copy. The cops' theory was that Henry had paid a large deposit for the painting, then when he realized it was fake, he flew into a rage and killed Osmond. And slashed the painting for good measure. They had matched the scalpel to Henry's old instrument case. Henry's fingerprints were on the scalpel.

"Of course they are," Henry said. "I used it for years."

Somehow this point seemed obvious only to him.

"And I never paid anything for the painting."

Don Quixote pursed his lips. "You wrote him a check for $200,000. Osmond deposited it the same day."

"That's impossible. I never wrote a check."

"Do you bank online?"

Henry nodded.

"Look at your account. You can probably bring up the check."

Henry hadn't looked at his account for a week. He logged onto the bank app on his cell. When he clicked on his accounts, he saw that $200,000 had been moved from his savings to his checking account, where a check for that amount had been written. He clicked to view the check: there it was, with his signature!

"I didn't write this. Someone forged my signature."

"Who would be able to do that?"

Henry shook his head, confused, desolate. He was trapped in a Dalí painting, one of those nightmarish landscapes where familiar images melted into the grotesque.

When they booked him, he called Suzy's cell and sobbed out the details.

"Calm down, little brother. I suppose you didn't do it."

"For pity's sake, Suzy! How can you even think it! Call Bernie and tell him to get down here."

"He's a corporate lawyer."

"Then find someone else! Don't tell Dad."

The next morning Henry went before a judge who denied him bail. The feeble arguments of the lawyer Suzy had found were demolished by the Crown, who pointed out that Henry had brought the scalpel to Osmond's apartment with the intent to kill.

He called Suzy again. "I don't know how but someone's framed me. You've got to help me."

"What can I do?"

"Remember the patient of mine who committed suicide a few months ago? I want you to call her husband, Mike Richmond. Don't tell him who you are. Tell him you're doing a survey for the hospital or something. Ask him if goes horseback riding. See if he'll admit to knowing Osmond."

He didn't like the silence on the other end of the line. "Please, Suzy."

He stewed in his cell for three weeks, calling Suzy collect every time they let him use the phone, only to hear she had no news. Finally, he was taken to the visitors' hall to meet with his lawyer, Mr. Pirelli. An elderly jowled man, with more hair sticking out of his nose than his head, he told Henry he'd had a phone meeting with the Crown to try to come up with a settlement. They had a tight case. But the lawyer argued that Henry had acted out of anger and could still be a useful member of society. The Crown was willing to reduce the charge from second degree murder, which carried a sentence of twenty-five years to life, to voluntary manslaughter if Henry pleaded guilty and spared them a trial. Jail time was a minimum ten years, but with good behavior he could be out in seven. If he wanted to go to trial, he would be waiting in jail for months. Probably years.

"I didn't do it!" Henry said.

Mr. Pirelli's jowls shook along with his head.

Henry leaned forward, lowering his voice. "My sister's looking into another lead. It might clear me."

"This deal is only on the table till tomorrow."

Henry called Suzy's cell in a panic. She said she had something to tell him and was on her way over.

He waited for her impatiently at the table in the visitors' hall, badly needing some good news. He was surprised when an elegant woman in a white suit and high heels walked toward him.

"Suzy?"

He took her hand but caught the approach of the guard and let it go. No touching allowed.

"You look different," he said.

She tilted her head. "I changed my hair. You like it?"

The longish brown hair he was used to had been cut short and spiky into a pale blonde bob. She looked younger, upbeat. Her cheeks glowed.

"Very becoming. You said you had news?"

Her greeting face tightened. "About Mike Richmond. He's not your guy. He's moved on, actually says he forgives you."

Henry had been counting on Richmond being the killer. "How do you know he's not lying? Maybe he forgives me now that I'm in jail for a murder he committed."

Suzy shook her head. "I don't think so. He seemed sincere. He sent his regards."

"I don't want his goddam regards!" Henry shouted. "I want him sitting here instead of me!"

The guard stepped toward them until Suzy held up a hand, signalling she had things under control.

"About that," she said. "Your lawyer asked me to talk to you about the plea deal. I think you should take it."

He rubbed his eyes, wishing the old Suzy would appear. "I'm not going to spend ten years in jail for something I didn't do."

"You could be out in five if you volunteer at the prison hospital." She looked down at her red-manicured nails. "You don't have to pretend with me, Henry."

"What do you mean? You think I did it?"

"These things happen."

"I can't believe it. You think I'm a murderer. I can prove my innocence. I want you to hire a private investigator."

"Look," she said, turning away her eyes, "I'm kind of busy. I have to sign some papers. Daddy wants me to take over the business."

She hadn't called him Daddy in years. "You told him?"

"He's very upset. He's taken your name off the board of directors. He finally realizes that I'm the best person to run the company. I have so many ideas where to take it. The company hasn't changed in decades—we could do so much more. China is a huge market..."

She went on and on until he was breathless. A black cloud expanded in his brain. "Suzy...I never wanted the company...I would've been happy with you taking over."

"Daddy would never have agreed. Now he has no choice."

Henry gaped at her. "Do you still go riding?"

"Sometimes."

His mouth twitched. "That's where you met Osmond..."

"The dead man?"

"You still have my house key?"

"I gave it back."

"No you didn't."

"Well, I haven't seen it for ages."

"Stop lying! You let yourself in and found the scalpel. And my check book. Both conveniently in my night table."

She blinked, her pretty face a mask.

"You never called Richmond, did you?"

"Now, little brother..."

"*You* were Osmond's client! You picked the perfect painting— you knew I couldn't resist it. How much did you pay him?"

She raised an eyebrow. "I don't know what you're talking about."

"What's my banking password?"

"How should I know?"

"Because you know me. It's the same password I use for everything. Mom's maiden name. You got into my account and moved the money. You forged my signature!"

He leaned over the table. "How could you do this to me? And you killed somebody..."

Her mouth set in a line, her face turned from him.

"I thought I knew you, but you're a stranger to me. My own sister!" He fleetingly thought of Angela, also a stranger, hiding her desperation from him. How could he have been so wrong about both of them? "You didn't have to do this…"

She glanced sideways at the guard then skewered Henry with fierce eyes. "You were always the golden boy who could do no wrong. Well, Daddy wants me to give you a message. He's cutting off your money…"

In a fog, Henry stood up, reached across the table and put his hands around her throat. He wanted to squeeze the life out of her. He didn't see the guards running toward them, or her contorted face turning red. All he saw were the cloaked figures in the painting, one treacherous, turning away, the other leaning in, punishing, both struggling upon the impenetrable heart.

"121" makes for Ben's second story to appear in the magazine after "A Calculated Risk" appeared back in issue two. In addition to his regular column in Mystery Scene *magazine and his western novels, this story is straight hard-boiled. I won't tell you what it's about or spoil any details but I will share a fragment from a sentence near the end of the story: "...hunched in the booth with a momentary stillness like an Edward Hopper painting waiting for its story to start." Because it's a real good line, that's why. And if you don't know the work of Edward Hopper...Jackson Pollock, too, if you want to be sure to get all the painter references. Hey, I'm just trying to help...*

121
Benjamin Boulden

"121" was painted unevenly in black across the faded red door, barely visible in the broken light.

The carpet was burnt orange, the walls were spackled and dirty, the cottage cheese ceiling just visible from the doorway. A fetid, musky odor brought bile up my throat and water to my eyes. Nothing more than a crummy room in a crummy motel, its only inhabitant a motionless detective, studying what was left of a woman.

As I entered the room Detective DeSpain looked away from the corpse, straight at me. He matched the room with his shabby brown suit and graying pornstache.

He said, "I thought you'd want to know."

"I appreciate it."

The dead woman sprawled on the floor, legs cloaked in shadow. The rest unblemished by clothes or modesty. A pool of blood spread across the cheap vinyl floor of the kitchenette from the back of her shattered head.

"You know her?" DeSpain's attention back on the girl.

"Maybe."

DeSpain twisted his head in a hurry, his eyes masked in shadow.

"What do you mean 'maybe'?"

"Half her face is gone, Greg," I said. "Maybe if the rest wasn't Pollocked on the wall I'd recognize her."

"Your boss know who she is?"

"You'd have to ask him."

"Where was he tonight?"

I stepped closer to the dead woman, concentrated on the gentle curve of her mouth, remembered that last time in my room. The sweet smell of chocolate and Chardonnay on her breath.

Dilated pupils, searching hands, the light and heavy play of lust and love.

Her name was Katherine, but she had preferred Katy. An old-fashioned name for a modern girl. A girl whose life ended with violence in a casino border town I thought of as my own. A girl I loved as much as a broken man can love anyone.

"Jenkins' latest, isn't she? Brought her from somewhere else?"

Jenkins operated the largest casino in town. A big man with big appetites. A throwback to the mob days of the 1950s and 1960s. He paid my rent, but I earned every nickel by keeping him and his casino clean.

And I risked the whole set-up by falling in love with his latest paramour.

"Everybody worth anything's from somewhere else," I said without looking away from Katy's mouth, the red lipstick still fresh on her lips. The sound of her voice already fading from memory.

DeSpain heard something in my words or thought he did since I could feel him staring. "You sure she isn't something to you?"

"Her?" I forced myself to meet DeSpain's gaze, control my blossoming rage. "I don't even know who she is. You get an ID, then ask."

DeSpain put a hand on my shoulder. "Know where Jenkins was tonight?"

A look of forced disbelief flashed across my face. "You think he did this?"

"I have to start somewhere. You know how it is."

"Yeah, I know how it is." And I did. Before I burned down my life, I was a special agent working the Salt Lake City office. Fraud, mostly, but I'd seen more than a few dead bodies. Kidnappings gone wrong, some bank robberies planned thirty seconds before the guns came out.

I said, "You'll have to ask Jenkins yourself since I got no idea where he was tonight."

"Sure." DeSpain grimaced, belched softly into a cupped hand.

"Where is everybody?"

"ME and crime scene's coming from Tooele," DeSpain said. "Otherwise it's just me." He stepped closer. "This is big. If Jenkins is involved, I need to know."

Tiring of the game I pulled a thin white envelope from my sports coat, held it up. "Thanks for calling." Then, with unwarranted hostility: "You want this?"

Anger flashed in DeSpain's eyes. "Jesus, man!" He furtively glanced at the motel room's exterior door. Its frame empty. He stepped toward me, grabbed the lapels of my coat and yanked so hard I nearly fell into him. "You *ever* try a handoff like that again you'll walk with a limp the rest of your life."

His breath was like the back side of a toilet.

I pushed him away. "You remember who pays your way."

DeSpain glowered, stuffed his hands in his pockets like a boy.

"You need to think hard before you start making accusations." My voice a whisper. "You want this or what?" I held the envelope toward him.

"Fuck you, Jimmy." He ripped the envelope from my hand.

Greg DeSpain's not a bad guy, he's not even that corrupt. He kept an eye out, comings and goings of known thugs, investigations initiated by my former employer, and anything else he thought would interest me. I paid him with Jenkins' roll, and he passed the money on to a special school where his autistic kid was enrolled. The tuition far outside a cop's reach.

The arrangement wouldn't protect me or the boss from a murder wrap but it was good enough to get me in the room before anyone else.

I turned and walked from the dingy motel room into the warm desert night. The lights of the Nevada casinos glowed on the western horizon. The Utah side had fallen dark in its shadow. The only thing on my mind was how Katy Miller had come to her violent end in a cut-rate rathole like the Moto-Valu. A girl too good for Wendover and Jenkins both. A girl too good for me.

***

I pulled into the gravel parking lot of Wanda's All-Nite Diner a few blocks south of Wendover Boulevard on First Street, parked next to the glass door. The boss's faux Jersey accent was in my ear. He showed no concern and even less surprise about Katy's condition.

"The Moto-Valu? What's she doing in that dump?" Amusement in his voice made me want to strike him.

"Her being your girl, I was hoping you'd know. When's the last time you saw her?"

"This an interrogation, Special Agent?"

"I'm only asking, but DeSpain will want something more formal."

Jenkins was silent a moment, his breathing sounded wet over the phone. "I ain't seen Katy in a week. Probably back on the game, picked up the wrong john."

"Sure."

"Yeah, 'sure.' Keep DeSpain away from me."

I slid the old-fashioned flip phone into my shirt pocket as I stepped from the car. I knew Jenkins was lying about when he'd last seen Katy and I had the feeling he'd known she was dead before I'd called. I was sure DeSpain hadn't gotten to him yet, meaning one of three things: he'd either killed Katy, knew who did, or my dislike for him was jading my judgment and I didn't know anything at all.

A bell clanged as I opened the door to empty booths and the abandoned counter. A small-town diner existing less because the food is edible and more because there was nowhere else to go unless you wanted mediocre, overpriced casino fare. And since most of the locals above a certain age worked in the casinos, no one wanted to spend their free time in the neon dusk unless they were either falling down drunk or addicted.

"With you in a second," a sweet feminine voice called from the back.

When she appeared, a few strands of hair escaped her ponytail and made her look younger than I knew her to be. Beautiful in that wholesome way, one that broke my heart with shame at who I had become. Or maybe what I had become. "Nice to see you, Jenny."

A nervous smile touched her large mouth. "Ford. Long time no see."

I gave her my best Robert Mitchum nod, practiced to perfection over the years. "You, too. Jenny—" She blurted something to stop me from finishing.

"Want some coffee?"

"To go, if you don't mind."

She gave me a disappointed look. "And I was hoping you came to see me."

I planted myself on a green-topped stool. "I did come to see you."

She raised her eyebrows, her forehead crinkled, the sides of her mouth curling upward. "Oh?"

"Seen your roommate recently?" Jenny and Katy were splitting costs at a mid-grade apartment on the Nevada side.

"Umm, yesterday. Why?" Jenny's mouth twitched, eyes cast downwards. She was a God-awful liar.

"Katy into something she shouldn't be?"

Jenny didn't answer right away. She turned away from me, pulled a coffee pot from its hotplate. A cardboard cup came off a tall stack and said, "Want anything in it?"

"Black's fine."

Jenny turned back and set the cup on the counter. "I don't know, Jimmy." She was talking about Katy again. "I haven't seen her much the past few weeks." She brushed a lock of wayward blonde away from her face. "I figured she was with you or Jenkins."

"Me?" I tried to sound surprised.

Jenny nodded. Her mouth a tight line, eyes gazing at her hands clenched on the scuffed Formica counter, body taut with tension.

"You know about Katy and me?"

She looked at me, sorrow in her pale blue eyes. "Katy told me."

I placed my hand on hers. "It's okay. No big secret." If Jenkins found out I'd been stroking the hen, trouble would come fast and hard. Maybe it already had and I didn't know it yet. "But she hasn't been around in a few days. I don't think Jenkins has, either."

"Is Katy in trouble?"

"Anyone unusual been hanging around?"

Jenny shook her head.

"New people in her life?"

Jenny paled. "Why—" She stopped, tilted her head. "A few days ago I came home early and there was a guy I hadn't seen before. He was sitting at the kitchen table like he came with the set."

"Yeah?"

"He was dressed nice. In a suit. But he didn't match his clothes."

"How's that?"

"His hands were beat up, rough and calloused. His knuckles puffy and bruised. Like maybe he'd been in a fight."

"What was he doing there?"

"I asked you already, but is Katy in trouble?"

"And I asked you what this guy was doing in your apartment."

She concentrated on my eyes a heartbeat. Her breathing was shallow, her face pale. A slight tremor in her hands. "I don't know but when Katy came out of the bedroom she was nervous. I thought it was because I caught her with a guy in our apartment." She stopped talking. A silver tear at the corner of an eye. "We have an agreement about that, you know. No men in the apartment. But she kept looking at him as we talked. When he left, she handed him an envelope. I didn't think much about it then but now I wonder if she owed him money."

My first thought was Katy had been acting as a go-between for Jenkins on some of his shady business.

I said, "Ever see him before?"

Jenny shook her head.

I dug deeper. "How'd he look?"

"Big guy. Unkempt red hair. Scars on his face, like he'd had acne as a teenager. An ugly flat nose."

I knew who Jenny was talking about. A freelance piece of garbage out of Salt Lake who'd recently been making a living as a heavy for the cartel. Kurt Mabry. It was concerning he was in town without me already knowing.

"And you think he was collecting a debt?"

She shook her head and leaned across the counter. "What's going on Jimmy? Is Katy in trouble?"

"She working?"

"What?" Jenny stepped back. "What do you mean?"

"Was she working it professionally?"

"No." A tear streamed down her left cheek. "At least I don't think so. You're scaring me, Jimmy. Please, is Katy in trouble?"

"Not anymore." I twisted on the stool and looked at my reflection in the window, Jenny behind me. My words sounded cruel but I wasn't trying to hurt her. "She's dead."

Jenny sobbed quietly as if she'd known it had to be so. "How?"

I unfolded myself from the stool and walked out the door. My coffee sat forgotten on the counter.

* * *

A decrepit single-story barracks, built like a shotgun shack, leaned on its foundation in line with five identical buildings. A relic from the old Army Air Corps training base built during the Second World War on Wendover's Utah side. Knee-high weeds swayed in the night breeze. A satellite dish attached to the roof above a white-washed door cast an oblong shadow in the dark. Windows dark, an elderly Chevy Lumina parked on scattered gravel a few feet away.

I moved quietly around the structure, looking for life in the surrounding buildings; lights, cars, noises. There was nothing besides the soft purr of the summer breeze and rise and ebb of chirping insects.

I approached the front door, climbed three wooden steps, pulled back the broken screen door. Paused to listen for any interior sounds. Unholstered the .38 from my belt and kicked next to the doorknob with the sole of my left foot. The cheap door splintered from the frame, crashing against the interior wall. Inside, I jagged to the left and crouched.

"What...who in...shit."

A shadowy figure, the headfirst and then lopsided shoulders popped against the wall. I stood, crossed the distance in three steps, grabbed the man's hair, pulled him to his feet. My revolver pressed into his jaw until it made a heavy O in his skin.

"Jesus," he whimpered. "Cool out, man."

"Shut up."

He jerked his head away from the .38. I hit him hard with the revolver's front sight, blood gushed from the soft flesh below his jawline.

He screamed and fell back against the wall. I released my grip, he tumbled to the floor.

I left him there, walked to the door, found the switch. The place popped into view under the dirty glow of a bulb hanging at the room's center from a frayed electrical cord. My eyes adjusted to the light; on the back wall I saw a makeshift kitchen, the bed on the right facing a television, and next to it a threadbare loveseat.

"Nice place."

Garvey—his name, and we were acquainted—squinting because of the light, said, "What?"

I stood over him, gun in hand and smiled.

"Mabry," I said. "Where is he?"

"Who?"

I kicked him in the stomach, let him moan a few seconds.

"Where is Kurt Mabry?"

"Ford?" My name sounded ugly and brutal in the dark room.

"Yeah, it's me," I said. "Mabry—where is he?"

He frowned. "Haven't seen him."

I grabbed him by the hair again, yanked him to his feet. He squealed, phlegm rattling in his throat.

"I have no patience. You tell me where Mabry is or I leave you in a pool of blood." I pointed to the kitchen floor. "Right there."

"What's wrong, Ford? We got no beef."

"Five," I counted. "Four...three—"

"Hold on, man. Mabry came to town a few days ago—Tuesday, I think. Yeah, man, Tuesday."

"Why?"

"Huh?"

"I said, why?"

"I don't know, man. He had some business."

"He still around?"

"Yeah. Sure. I think so."

"Where?"

"How am I supposed to know?"

I brought my knee into his crotch. A rush of air exploded from his mouth. His eyes popped wide, then clamped shut.

Wheezing, Garvey grabbed himself with both hands. Before he could fall I gripped his shirt front, pushed him against the wall, crowded close, the business end of the .38 hard into his stomach. "I thought you could tell I'm not playing. Now where's Mabry?"

"The Boulevard. At the Moto."

Garvey fell to his knees when I stepped away.

"Why's he in town? What's he doing?"

"I got no business with him. He calls and tells me to meet at the Garter for lunch on Tuesday."

"Yeah?"

"Yeah, nothing. That's it. We shoot the shit, talking old days and better pay. That's it, man." He stared up at me. Blood trickled down his neck where the front sight of my S&W had slashed his flesh.

"The cartel moving into town?"

Garvey's eyes bugged from his head. "I don't know, man. I'm a nothing. A scrounger, you know that."

"Our deal, in case you forgot, is that you tell me when something unusual is happening. Then I keep a blind eye to your lesser scams."

"A visit from an old buddy, that's all. We had lunch, nothing more."

I shook my head. "It's time for you to go."

He looked up, pain and confusion in his eyes.

"Out of town. I see you again, I'll find a shallow hole on the Silver Islands and roll your corpse into it. You're done here."

"Sure," he whispered. "Yeah. I was going to fly this coop anyway."

I watched him a moment, writhing on the floor. Gasping for breath. I turned and walked into the moonless night, back to my car. As I pulled away Garvey's shadow appeared in the doorway.

I was worried I could be losing it and I was feeling out of control. All I could think about was Katy's crumpled and broken body. Her low, sexy laugh and that way she would look up at me with glimmering promise and temptation in those amazing green eyes. I could hear the inane words I used as I walked out her door that last time. I wanted to remember telling her she was everything to me. That I loved her, but I knew my parting words would have been clinical and meaningless: "See you later" or "Take care" or even worse, "Stay beautiful."

I parked two blocks from the Moto-Valu Motel on a dark section of street. The air crisp on my face as the day's heat faded from the desert landscape. The motel was a flurry of activity. Crime scene technicians moved in and out of Katy's ground floor room. A scattering of sightseers stood at the outside edges of the yellow tape, leaning over the balcony of the second floor to get a glimpse of something dead. DeSpain's black LTD had been joined by an unmarked van, probably the crime scene unit, a white, blue and black West Wendover police cruiser and a Tooele County Fire Department ambulance.

Avoiding attention, I moved along the edges of the crowd, never looking toward Katy's room, aiming for the motel's office. I passed a young family. The father pointed toward the open doorway of 121: "...in there, I bet."

His wife, young and Mormon, a recognizable smugness in her

voice, "Probably a hooker." A girl, maybe eight, silently watched the activity.

I pushed through the office door, the desk man looked up from the telephone, a grin on his face, excitement gleaming in his eyes. "I got to go," he said into the mouthpiece. Then, to me, "Quite a night."

"What happened?"

"Murder." The man's smile glowed. His name tag read, *Todd J, Night Manager*. "Right here, in one of my rooms."

"Yeah?" I stepped to the counter, leaned against its faux wood and Formica top, tried to conceal the rage tearing me up. "Who was it?"

His gaze glanced over my right shoulder. "A woman."

"A guest?"

"Umm, yeah. Checked in yesterday. Good-looking babe. Blonde, real hot." Todd put his hands up to his chest, pantomiming breasts. "Tits out to here, man."

I leaned in closer. "You know her name?"

"Uhh—" He stopped suddenly. "You a cop or something?"

I shook my head. "Curious is all."

His smile came back. "Yeah. Sure. Me too. Curious, I mean."

"Well?"

"Look, man." Todd made eye contact for the first time, his pupils unfocused and hazy, probably from a low-grade meth addiction. "Can I do something for you?"

"Sure, you can. I'm looking for Kurt Mabry. He's staying here but he didn't give me his room number."

Todd stared blankly. He wanted to get back to the activities outside instead of listening to me.

"Tall. Red hair, sharp clothes."

Todd looked over my shoulder again.

I reached out and slapped his face. "You with me, Todd?"

His head jerked back from the impact, eyes widened. "Did you—"

Leaning over the counter I whispered, "You need to do your job, Todd. I need to find my friend. Mr. Mabry. Red hair, ugly, big flat nose." I straightened up, looked Todd in his teared-up eyes. "Do you think you can help me?"

"Yeah." His furtive brown eyes looking for help outside the office windows, then drifting back to me, defeated. "I can. I know who you're talking about. Mr. Mabry. Checked in Tuesday, scheduled to

113

leave tomorrow."

"What room?"

"Two-oh-two." Todd's voice quavered.

"See how good service works, Todd? Room two-oh-two, you said?"

He nodded. Everything forgotten except our conversation.

"I'm planning to surprise my friend—" I rapped the counter with my knuckles, "—and if you ruin it for me I'll have to come back."

Todd's Adam's apple bounced, head shaking nervously. He stepped backwards until the wall stopped him. I didn't feel any pity for the ghoul. Todd deserved everything I did to him.

The motel's backside was surprisingly quiet for the night's activity as neighboring casinos lit the horizon with an eerie, hard glow. Traffic flashed past on I-80 with rhythms of red and white, screaming tires and thrumming engines. Listening intently, my ear close to the door of room 202, I pushed away the other sounds. A television blaring from within, a phony sitcom laugh track. An indistinct one-sided conversation, Mabry talking to himself or someone else I couldn't hear. Then nothing except the television and a barely discernible squeaking.

I adjusted the gun in my right hand, took a step back, and stood straight and square to the door. A deep breath cooled my nerves. I rapped the steel with my knuckles. The noise of the television evaporated. The interior fell silent except for the squeaking I'd heard earlier and now realized were the protesting floorboards under a man's shifting weight. Then footsteps as the room's occupant approached the door. Nothing more for a few beats as I imagined Mabry listening, nervous, on his side of the door.

"Yeah?" he finally said, barely loud enough to hear.

"Wendover PD," I said. "We'd like to have a word with you, sir."

"What about?" His voice louder, more assured.

I grimaced—*what about?*—and said, "Some trouble earlier tonight in another room. We're canvassing for witnesses."

"Don't know what you're talking about."

"Please open the door, sir. We have a few questions, then we'll leave you to your night." I paused, counted to three. "Otherwise, the manager will open the door."

A whispered expletive. Then: "Sure, give me a sec."

I took a short step back, another to the right for the best angle at the door's right-hand swing. Adjusted my feet into a wide stance, the left slightly forward from the right, knees bent, held the revolver in both hands, aimed a foot above the door's threshold and waited for it to open.

Ten, fifteen, twenty seconds passed. My heart thundered, pounding my ears and engorging the veins along my neck. I forced myself to concentrate, watch the door for movement, listen for the sounds—

Deadbolt clicked.

Door knob turned.

I blinked once, held my breath as a crack of light flashed between door and jamb. With my left foot, I kicked the door below the knob. The security chain held for a moment before snapping. Mabry took the door's impact on his right shoulder. He stepped back and cursed.

I caught the door with my left shoulder as it swung back toward the frame, propelling it inward again and brought the revolver high and smashed it downward on Mabry's skull with a thud. Mabry slumped to the floor. His two hundred pounds crashed on the forty-year-old flooring. Blood staining his scalp as it dripped to the faded orange carpet.

Stepping back, I watched the prone man for a moment and then quickly assessed the room. Empty, except for an ancient television with Zenith's name on its black casing, a bed with a dilapidated nightstand next to it. At the back was a gold-flecked mirror and sink, milky plastic cups still in their wrappings stacked in a column. A doorway to the right opened to the toilet.

I moved through the room in a hurry, checking for unwelcome guests, but found no one except the still unconscious Kurt Mabry.

The .38 back in its holster, I closed the room's door and locked the deadbolt. I dragged Mabry into the bathroom, handcuffing his wrists around the toilet's base and manacled his ankles with another pair.

I splashed Mabry's ugly face with water from an ice bucket.

Mabry gasped. His eyes flickered open with pain and confusion. He tugged at the constraints on his wrists—the toilet not budging— and helplessly tried to get traction with his feet before he noticed me standing outside the bathroom door.

"The fuck?"

"That about sums up your future, Mabry."

Looking tough with a dented head and your arms wrapped around a toilet is difficult, but Mabry gave it his best.

"The way I see it—" I pushed myself away from the vanity to the bathroom doorway, "—we can play games. You can keep yourself to yourself and I can beat you to death." I tapped the bottom of his left foot with the toe of my right. "Or you can answer a few questions and we both leave here without any more bruises."

"What the hell do you want?"

"Why are you here?"

"The shit you care?"

I filled the ice bucket from the toilet and dumped more water on his face. He sputtered and cursed. Then, finally, "Fuck you."

I leaned against the door jamb. Pulled a thin white towel from a rusty shelf, twisted it into a tight cylinder. "In the long ago I worked in Iraq. Back in the good days when we were free to do what we wanted. And I tell you, they taught us some twisted stuff. They called it 'enhanced interrogation' but—and this is between you and me—it was straight up torture."

I held the towel at chest height, twisting it tighter.

"Take this towel. I can do more with it than you can imagine. The easiest and most popular is waterboarding. I place this towel over your face, pour water into it. You probably won't drown, but when I'm through you'll wish you had."

Mabry's eyes widened as he watched the towel in my hands.

"We'll keep it simple. Waterboarding's damned easy for me. So far you don't need to know about our other options—"

I pulled another towel from the rack. "I should have mentioned, to do it right you need two." Then, pointing to the ice bucket, "And that."

Mabry shuddered. "N-no. No...please. I had a buddy over there—"

I sat on my heels, leaned closer to Mabry. "So I asked you, why are you here?"

He hesitated. I raised the towel in my right hand.

"Okay. Okay, yeah."

I let him talk a moment, allowing his tongue to get comfortable moving. Then, "Why Wendover? We're not worth a cartel heavy visiting—even freelance trash like you."

He gulped, breath caught in his throat. "I—Routine, man. Nothing special, really. I came to scare a bitch."

"Watch your language. Who was it?"

"A mule." He lifted his head off the cold tile. I pushed it back. "Yeah?"

"Just a mule. She was having trouble with a—her roommate. She'd found out. The roommate found out what our mule was doing." Mabry was getting into the story, worrying about me and not the death sentence he was earning from his employer. "She was mumbling about calling the cops."

My breath caught. I tried to figure why Katy would mule drugs for the cartel. "You killed her?"

"Which one?"

"The mule."

"No, man. I didn't kill nobody. Threatened her is all I did."

"The mule?"

He looked at me, puzzled. "Why would they want me to threaten the mule?"

The light bulb flashed, slower than I liked, but it flashed all the same. The rage leeched away, replaced by an empty tiredness that felt as much like loneliness as anything I'd ever known.

After finding the apartment Katy and Jenny shared dark and empty, I went to Wanda's. If anything, it looked even more forlorn than it had earlier. The surrounding houses and buildings were dark, the diner's windows lighted white and yellow against the ink of night. The booths and tables vacant. Jenny, cleaning the counter, looked up as I parked my car in a space next to the door. She quietly waved and went back to work with the rag in her hand. I sat and watched for a moment, then made a call to my boss and Katy's keeper, Jenkins.

"You should have told me."

"About?"

"The cartel. Moving smack into town."

"You work for me," Jenkins said. "I decide what you're told or not told. I thought you'd figure it out since I pay you to know that kind of thing."

"You know Kurt Mabry?"

"No."

"Works freelance for the cartel?"

"Still don't know him."

"You know why he's in town?"

"No. Why's he in town?" His voice sarcastic, insolent.

"How'd you know Katy was dead before we talked?"

"I didn't. What's this got to do with Mabry?"

"The cartel sent him to Wendover to deal with a problem."

Silence.

"Sent him to deal with Katy, but you already knew that, right?"

"Sure." His voice tinny in my ear. Quiet. "He kill her?"

"Was he supposed to kill her?"

"That wasn't part of the play. I liked Katy."

I listened to the fat man's breathing for a few seconds before disconnecting the call. He knew the cartel was bringing drugs into Wendover and he didn't care so long as his casino looked clean and he got his cut. Worse, he allowed a cartel goon to play in our house, muscle Katy and the whole time kept me in the dark.

The bell jangled as I opened the door to Wanda's. Jenny looked up.

"I thought you'd be back." Her face drawn tight, mouth a straight line, eyes red like she'd been crying.

"I figured you'd go home."

"It's easier to work than think. About Katy, I mean."

I nodded.

"Busy?" I motioned toward a booth.

"You want coffee? You forgot to take it last time."

"Sure." I took a green vinyl-covered booth, watching as Jenny filled a mug.

She set it on the table in front of me.

We sat in silence for a few minutes. Me watching the coffee, Jenny alternating between staring at her hands, me, and our reflection in the night shrouded window.

"You figured it out, didn't you?" A tear streamed down her cheek. Her hands shook uncontrollably in her lap.

I reached across the table, wiped away the stain. "Why?"

She sobbed. "I didn't want to. You have to know that. Please. You have to." Jenny's face pale with anguish, her voice heavy with fear. "She wouldn't—wouldn't listen. They'll kill him if I stop." She reached across the table, grasped my left hand in hers. "They really will. If anything happens, they'll kill him."

"Who will they kill, Jenny?"

"If I'm caught. If I can't bring the drugs in."

"Who are you talking about, Jenny?"

"They—" She hesitated. "My brother. He—he's an addict. They own him. He owes the cartel money."

Jenny. The good girl. A cartel mule, hauling smack from Salt Lake City to this outpost of casinos pretending to be a town. The woman who made me feel shame for my disgrace was blackened with her own.

My anger rose at the kind of world that would use Jenny's love for her brother as a wedge for corruption.

"Why Katy?"

"She—" Jenny looked at me with hate-filled eyes, hate for herself at what she'd done. "Katy wouldn't listen, wouldn't understand."

"Did she tell someone? About you?"

She pulled her hands away from mine. "She threatened to tell you, Jimmy."

The breath caught in my throat. My eyes burned. I remembered the story Katy told me a few weeks earlier about her mother. About how Katy found her dead, the needle still in her arm, face twisted in fear and pain. An impotent rage flared cold at the back of my skull. If I'd been told before everything fell apart, Katy would be alive and Jenny could walk away free.

But now everything was useless, spoiled.

"Who did you tell?"

"A number. They gave me a number to call for trouble. They sent that man. The red-haired man. He said he would take care of everything. But she wouldn't listen."

"Why the Moto? Why there?"

"I asked her to meet me. To talk. I didn't think anyone would know us. Me or Katy. I didn't mean it to happen." A fluorescent light in the spotted ceiling caught her attention. "The gun, it just came out..."

"What about Jenkins?"

Jenny paused. Her face red and blotchy, mouth open. "What?"

"Did he know?"

"About me?"

"About Katy. Did he want you to kill her?"

She shook her head.

"Me. It was me." Her eyes red, mascara streaked at the corners, hands and head trembling. "I'm sorry, Jimmy. I'm so sorry."

We sat for a few minutes, the only sound Jenny's sobbing. I reached across the table, squeezed her hand, stood and walked away, the glass door swinging behind me, the cold starry night ahead. Katy dead, Jenny destroyed and her junkie brother alive, breathing, making a mess no one else could clean up.

Then I was in my car, backing away from Wanda's, Jenny hunched in the booth with a momentary stillness like an Edward Hopper painting waiting for its story to start.

I turned on to the emptiness of the early morning Boulevard, toward Nevada and the casino, where Jenkins kept his rooms on the penthouse floor.

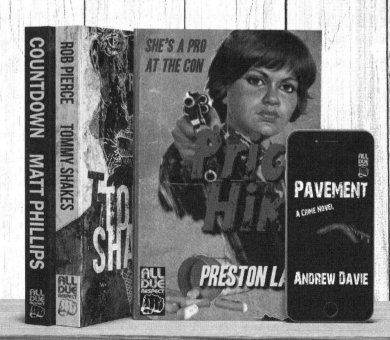

Experienced traveler and military vet, Dane Baylis is no stranger to literary magazines from both the United States and Canada. The story we have here is straight-ahead crime fiction, complete with nasty people from, shall we say, different walks of life, coming together for a period of time, working for the common good. Yeah, sure. Good old-fashioned teamwork. But where's the fun in that, especially in this genre? You'll find out…

Debts
Dane F. Baylis

From that first trip to Lyman School for Boys at age thirteen, Jimmy Kelly knew there were fights he was never going to win, but he'd have to show up for them anyway. The Cleary twins had asked him to keep an eye on a crumpled paper sack while they ducked into a restaurant to use the toilet. When Williams, the beat cop, grabbed him a moment later he knew the Cleary's had literally left him holding the bag. One that contained three stolen handguns. Even so, his fear of the twins outweighed his fear of the law.

In South Boston silence in a bad situation was the rule. In the face of his reticence the court was no more sympathetic than the cops. Barely into his teens, Jimmy pulled two years in lock-up and a reputation as a "stand-up guy," the type who could be counted on to take the fall. This earned him his bones and a life spent in the revolving door of the Massachusetts Correctional System.

But this time it was different game. Beginning with a phone call at two-thirty a.m., an hour he knew probably didn't contain an invitation to the ball. As he sat at Irene's kitchen table watching the sky outside the window change from black to gray and then a faintly sanguine blue, he wondered if there was any way he could win this one.

A bare bulb in the ceiling fixture highlighted the lines in Irene's face as she sipped from her Seven and Seven. "I swear to Christ, Kelly, I don't know what I'm gonna do." She stared at the ice in her glass. "I got unemployment coming and I guess that'll keep the roof over my head, but I can't afford no goddamned doctors."

Kelly's eyes hadn't left the mug of tea between his hands. "Finding out you got them tumors is a rough call, babe. That prick had no cause to let you go like that."

"I've been sick an awful lot, Jimmy. At least Sully laid me off and didn't can me. That would have meant a ten-week waiting period before I'd even get a check." She tossed the drink back and cleared her throat. "Ten weeks with no bennies? I'd be in the street faster than a change in Cape Cod weather."

Kelly looked at her through eyes only a shade or two bluer than the morning sky. "Not if I've got anything to say about it, Reenie girl." He checked the kitchen clock and said, "I have to meet some guys about work. If I don't get too tied up, I'll drop by tonight. If that's okay...?"

Irene stood to see him out and gave his shoulder a squeeze. "The door's always open for you, Jimmy. In forty-two years have I ever turned you away?"

He got up to leave and gave her a tight smile and a wink. "Not a once, sweetie."

In the stairwell's gloom he waited to hear the deadbolt snap then headed downstairs and through the basement passage to the street. Outside he paused and checked as much of the morning traffic as he could see, then ascended to the sidewalk. G Street was quiet and would remain that way for another half hour before neighborhood kids would start to scuff and holler their way to school. This early, anything unusual would stand out. Nothing did, so Kelly turned his collar against the December wind and moved on.

He legged it over to Perkins Square where the foot traffic was already heavy and he blended with the crowd. Popping into Dunkin' Donuts for a cruller and a coffee Kelly took a seat by the window. Before he could settle in, his ride pulled up. Leaving the cruller, he carried the waxed paper cup with him as he squeezed into the cramped back seat of Billy Flynn's flame red Camaro. Before Kelly sat back, Flynn hit the gas and, tires smoking and squealing, bulled his way into traffic. Kelly was still reaching for his seatbelt when the sudden lurch of the car nearly caused him to dump the still-steaming coffee in the lap of his fellow back seat passenger.

"What's your goddamned hurry, Flynn?" growled Kelly over the crude, barely intelligible hip-hop rumbling from speakers long since fried by decibel levels they were never meant to handle.

The young man behind the wheel glanced at him in the rearview mirror and quipped, "Relax, Jimmy. I got it handled."

Kelly wasn't placated and as he finished buckling in, coffee somehow intact, countered, "Getting pulled over this morning would be your idea of handled?"

"What? I got no points on my license. Everybody here's clean. We're just four guys on our way to work. Cops got more important things to do."

Tommy Boyle looked at Kelly from the other side of the front seat. "Don't be an old woman, Jimmy." Compared to the other three, the "old" part of what Boyle said was truer than Kelly wanted to admit.

He eyed the guy in the back with him and noticed his fingers drumming a quick tattoo against the side panel. Thinking to lighten the mood, Kelly asked, "You okay, Devlin?"

The young guy's eyes darted to Kelly. "Yeah, I'm okay. Why?"

Kelly wiggled his fingers in the air, an imitation of Devlin's drumming.

"I'm just hyped…ready to get this done."

Kelly nodded. "Thought it might be nerves, being your first time and all."

"What would you know?"

Boyle piped in from up front. "Jimmy's a veteran, Devlin. He's got as much time inside as you are old."

"No shit? Twenty years in the joint? Why's he here then? I thought the idea was to not get caught?"

Kelly sighed. "Yeah, well, things don't always work out like they're supposed to."

Flynn joined the exchange, "Jimmy took the fall for a job he did with my Uncle Sean. That's why I brought him in. Sean says he's stand-up all the way and knows his stuff. End of discussion."

"We should have stuck with the Charlestown guys." Devlin huffed and slouched into his corner of the back seat. So much for lightening the mood.

Flynn's voice hardened. "It's my plan. I brought him in and that's that."

Kelly tuned out the discussion. He had other things on his mind.

Truth was, that Russian bastard Nikolai down in Rhode Island had put him up to this. Kelly owed Nicky's brother for helping him make it through that last stretch in Souza-Baranowski Correctional but the real decider had been when Irene first dropped her news on him. For different reasons he owed them both.

A quick trip down Elkins Street brought them to the old warehouse where Kelly had stashed the utility van he'd had done up to look like an Edison maintenance vehicle. He keyed a remote for the roll-up door and they pulled the car inside. As the others climbed out Kelly asked Flynn, "Did you bring everything?"

The younger guy popped the trunk of the Camaro and fished out a box of latex gloves. Kelly passed them around, saying, "From this point on, no one touches anything without these." Pulling on two pair, he dragged a polyethylene tarp off the van, fished the vehicle's keys from his pocket and opened the doors. Leaning inside he dug out coveralls, hard hats, and black knit caps, passing them to the others. "There's one set for each of us. We'll put our personal hats, jackets, and any ID in the trunk of the car along with the tarp. They stay here until we come back."

"What if somebody...doesn't come back?" Devlin asked.

"Then he was never here. The others get rid of his stuff," Kelly replied, trying to hide his irritation.

Flynn snorted. "Fair enough."

After everyone had changed clothes Kelly pulled a duffel bag out of the Camaro's trunk. This held three empty canvas gym bags, four handguns and a cell phone for each of them. As he distributed the contents and tossed the duffel back in the trunk, Flynn asked, "You're sure these shooters are okay?"

"Yeah, I'm sure," Kelly answered, his breath catching at the sound of the slide on a pistol being racked next to his ear. Looking over his shoulder he found himself staring down the barrel of the piece he'd just handed Flynn.

"How sure is sure?"

Kelly's face showed nothing as he reached out slowly and pushed the barrel gently to his left. "Yeah. Real sure."

Flynn's eyes were ice as he laughed. Without another word he released the hammer and stuffed the piece behind his waistband. Looking at the others he barked, "Well, then. Let's get this done."

Boyle and Devlin, unsettled, laughed at their leader's joke as they, too, put their weapons out of sight. Armed and disguised, they climbed into the back of the van. Flynn took the wheel and Kelly, still showing no more disturbance than a frozen lake, took shotgun. He hit the button on the remote and the warehouse door rolled up so they could pull out. No one could see Kelly's hand shaking inside his pocket.

They cruised across Fort Point channel and picked up Route Three. For it being midweek the traffic wasn't so bad as they turned toward the North Shore and Revere. Devlin resumed his nervous tapping while Boyle and Flynn sang along with some gangsta crap on the radio. Kelly opened the glove box where he'd stashed a battery powered police scanner. He inserted an ear bud and monitored the chatter as they rolled toward the job. Distracted, his breathing calmed as his temper cooled. On the grand scale of things this was nothing compared to what Irene's battles must be like.

Leaving the highway, they pulled into the parking lot of the Massachusetts Mutual Bank near the old greyhound track. This had been a fairly active area back when the course was open but now most of it had been converted to light industrial. Residential traffic was almost non-existent. Flynn swung the SUV around the perimeter of the asphalt so they could look for anything different from yesterday's visit. Nothing had changed.

He parked next to the power pole that carried a connector box for the bank alarm system. Kelly got out with him while the other two remained in the back of the van. The younger man pulled a ladder down from the roof rack and extended it high enough to reach the pole steps while Kelly opened the side door on the van just enough to remove a tool belt and weather shroud. Flynn looked around the empty lot and with a nervous cough, said, "Okay, sport. Get upstairs and work your magic."

Kelly grunted as he strapped on the tools, slung the canvas over his shoulder, and carried it all up the ladder. Once on top, he arranged the shroud so he'd be shielded from the view of passing traffic and anyone in the parking lot below. Satisfied with his cover, he pulled a cordless screwdriver from his belt and had the lid to the alarm box off in under fifteen seconds. It took a few more to identify the terminals he needed. He pulled a printed circuit board from his coat pocket and pressed its power button. A red LED on its corner glowed then blinked every five seconds as it searched for a signal. He double-checked the alarm systems feeds and attached them by alligator clips to the terminals on his board.

He jumped a bit when his phone vibrated. He answered it and heard Flynn's voice: "How's it going?"

"We're all set." Jimmy checked his connections once more and settled in to wait. The day had clouded up and a raw, damp breeze blew through his perch. He pulled a pair of workman's gloves over his latex ones, tightened the cuffs and collar on his Edison company jacket and settled in. There wouldn't be long to wait.

A red 5 Series BMW slipped into the parking space marked "Manager." As Kelly watched, a middle-aged guy in a high-dollar suit and sunglasses climbed out. He spotted the van by the bank entrance and hesitated before approaching.

"Uh, what's going on?"

Flynn made a show out of steadying the ladder as Kelly played around with his tools. "Could be a problem with the transformer, chief. We might have to swap it out. Know for sure when we finish our tests."

The suit seemed to think this over. "I didn't know we were having any problems."

"All I know is we got a work order to check it out. Probably nothing more than loose connections."

"They usually send out a notification to customers if there's a problem. Don't they?"

"Go figure, eh? We'll be done pretty quick. There's a boom truck on stand-by in case we have to make a switch."

"So—we might lose power?"

"Yeah, but you've got backup, right?"

"Yes, we do. Well..." The suit extended his hand. There was a card between his fingers. "That's me. The phone number is direct to my office."

Flynn took the proffered card and touching the bill of his hard hat smiled his cold smile. "You'll know everything we're doing, boss."

Entering through the front door of the building, the suit locked it behind him. A few minutes later Kelly watched the LED on his board go from red to yellow, the signal the manager had switched the alarm to safe mode. Everything was now in place as the other employees began arriving.

The bank was scheduled to open in twenty minutes and the time lock would tumble ten minutes before that. It was the assistant manager's habit to arrive just before the lock clicked. Today she would be Flynn and the crew's key in.

The waiting part wasn't good for Kelly. His thoughts kept turning to Irene. So long as things went as they'd rehearsed his cut of the job would help with her medical bills. If there was some other way to come up with that much money, he'd have done it—but he was an ex-con and this was how he knew to do things. There simply weren't that many doors open to him.

Kelly hit speed dial and Flynn answered. "We still set?"

"Yeah. He just switched the alarm. Remember, in and out in seven minutes. Stick to the plan."

"So long as nobody gets brave or stupid, we're good."

"Boyle putting a round in the ceiling should convince them one way or the other."

The line went dead and Kelly shivered as he watched the employee section of the lot continue to fill up. Finally, the silver Mercedes he'd been looking for rolled into a reserved spot and a good-looking woman in her mid-thirties climbed out. Kelly watched the assistant manager walk toward the building as he picked up his phone and hit the speed-dial again. This time Boyle's phone vibrated to let him and Devlin know she was here.

As the woman passed Flynn he turned, grabbed her collar and hissed into her ear, "Nice and calm, sister. Open the door." He backed up the order with the cold pressure of his gun barrel pressed into the back of her neck. She fumbled her key into the lock and out of the corner of her eye, saw two more men slip in behind them.

Kelly saw their move from above and flipped a switch on the circuit board. The LED went from yellow to green. The interrupter was now sending a phony safe mode signal to the alarm company. Even if the employees inside tripped the silent its signal wouldn't make it past Kelly's gizmo.

The hostage worked the lock and Flynn shoved her inside and down onto the carpet. Boyle leaped over them. He raised the pistol in his hand over his head and it bucked. The shot, sounding like an explosion as it bounced off the walls, sent plaster dust raining down on them. Every face in the building snapped in the direction of the commotion. Boyle and Devlin wasted no time. They swung their own weapons toward the employees, yelling for everyone to lie face down on the floor. The door swung shut and Devlin snatched the keys from the assistant manager's hand and locked it. From his perch outside on the pole Kelly heard the shot and cut the wires for the land lines.

Next, Kelly calmly stripped the weather shroud and dropped it behind the van. He hustled down the ladder and once on the ground stuffed tools and canvas into the vehicle before securing the ladder in its rack. He checked his watch—just over two minutes gone. He scanned the parking lot and took deep, controlled breaths as the second hand on his watch crept around, praying the men inside the bank would keep to schedule.

Three minutes gone. He speed-dialed Flynn's number, using the buzz of the vibrator to prod things along. He checked the area around the pole to make sure he hadn't forgotten anything and climbed into the driver's seat.

Five minutes. He speed-dialed once more. On the outside he looked like a worker chilling on a break. Inside he was anything but relaxed. What if something went wrong? What if someone did get brave in there and one of the crew freaked and turned a pistol on them? That kid, Devlin, was supposed to gather up all the employees' cell phones. What if he missed one and a call got out somehow? Kelly's eyes bounced between the view through the windshield and the one from each mirror.

Seven minutes gone. He hit speed-dial again. This was the signal to finish and get out. Through the doors he saw them headed his way. Each carried a stuffed bag over his shoulder. Kelly tapped a different digit into the phone's memory then closed the line and turned the key in the ignition. As they cleared the building Devlin locked the bank door. Moving quickly without running they all piled into the van. Kelly put it in gear and pulled out of the parking lot, smooth and easy.

From the passenger seat, Flynn yelled, "C'mon, old man, step on it!"

Kelly barked back, "Taking a chance at getting pulled over on the way to a heist wasn't bad enough? You want to get us pinched leaving one?"

Flynn pointed his piece at Kelly's mid-section. "I said drive, son of a bitch."

Kelly's eyes never left the road. "Go ahead, tough guy. Pull the trigger. Then who steers?"

Boyle spoke up from the back. "Flynn! Chill! We got in and out without a hitch. Let's stick to our plan. Okay?"

Flynn didn't move right away. Then he slowly lowered the automatic. "You're right, kid. Stick to the plan. It's just the adrenaline rush." His smile returned. "Hey! No hard feelings. Right, Kelly?"

Kelly watched the cars ahead as he swung onto Route One and headed toward Chelsea. That was twice with this guy now. His knuckles were white as he gripped the wheel. "Yeah, stick to the plan," he muttered as he eased into the morning traffic and listened to the portable scanner. Looking in the rearview mirror, he said, "Devlin, you locked everybody in the supply closet, right?"

The young guy held up the assistant manager's keys and smiled as he jingled them. "Everybody."

"What about the phones?"

Devlin slapped his palm to his forehead. "The goddamn cell phones."

Kelly shot him a look. "You're shitting me, right?"

The kid laughed as he dug into his pockets and several phones clattered to the bare metal floor. "Fuck! You should see the look on your face."

"Never mind my looks. Pull the batteries and SIM cards out of those, put all the pieces in a bag, and smash all of it."

Devlin went to work with enthusiasm. Kelly tossed him the phone he'd used. "That one, too," he said, and then to Flynn and Boyle, "and both of yours. Everything gets busted and burned. It won't stop the cops from tracing some parts of the circuit boards and cases, but it'll slow them down." They handed over their phones then stripped off the crew jackets, knit caps and hard hats. All of it would burn with the van.

They exited the expressway and Kelly guided them along surface streets to Everett. The mix of traffic in the industrial area along the Mystic River was good cover. He eventually turned onto Chemical Lane and eased into some bushes next to a rail line behind an empty big box store.

"End of the line." He shut off the motor and climbed out. "The switch car's parked in row C-5 in front of the store. The gray Camry Boyle boosted three days ago. It's sporting the Connecticut plates I picked up for it now." He nodded toward the tracks as he shrugged off his coverall and tossed it into the van through the back door.

Boyle and Devlin followed his lead and stood near the back of the van. "Good planning," Flynn added. "Good choice of words, too. End of the line. It fits." He leveled his gun at Kelly's chest. "Now toss me the keys."

Kelly grabbed for the piece in his waist band, knowing he couldn't hope to beat the younger man's reflexes. As his own fingers closed around his gun butt, he heard the hammer on Flynn's snap as the young guy squeezed off a shot. The look on the punk's face was priceless. First that sadistic sneer and then, when there was no roar or recoil, pure panic.

Kelly drew his pistol. "Yeah, Flynn, that's right. Good Planning." His finger tightened on the trigger and this time there was the expected report. His adversary crumpled to the ground, a red hole in the middle of his forehead. When they heard the shot, the other gang members spun around and brought their guns to bear. Kelly didn't flinch as their weapons also failed to fire. Both men had pulled their triggers on dummy rounds. Raising his pistol, Kelly was surprised by a sudden ripple of muffled automatic weapons fire from the nearby bushes.

His two remaining accomplices seemed to be taken by seizures. When the staccato sound stopped, they were on the ground oozing blood. As the shooters stepped from cover, Kelly tucked his pistol back in his belt. The two in the lead slipped silenced Mac 11s back inside their overcoats as they advanced. The third calmly lit a cigar.

"So, Kelly," called the smoker, "just as I told you. This Flynn is a real pig, eh?" Passing the lifeless body, he spat and added, "By the way, nice shot."

"Lucky is all, Nick," Kelly replied, "and amateurism on their part. Never trust someone else to buy your ammo or load your gun. Boyle's magazine had the only other live round. Just the one—to scare the bank employees into cooperating."

Nikolai pulled the bags full of money from the side door of the van as his shooters hefted the corpses into the back. He signaled toward the railroad crossing and a black SUV rolled up alongside the vehicle.

"So, one for you," Nikolai dropped a bag of cash at Kelly's feet, "and two for me. That covers your services and repays what your ex-partner stole from me. That makes us straight, yes?"

"Of course." Keeping an eye on Nikolai's men, Kelly patted Flynn down until he found the hood's car keys. He'd made arrangements to have that hopped up Camaro put into a container bound for Singapore that night. He saw it as value added for all the threats he'd endured and the loud-mouthed clown's attempted betrayal. Kelly had let it go cheap, but he was able to expedite the deal that way. Next, he pulled a plastic jerry can full of gas and a roadside emergency flare from the back of the getaway truck. Items it seemed Flynn had intended using on him. Kelly splashed the liquid all over the interior and its contents then tossed in the can itself.

He waited long enough for Nicky and his crew to climb into their Escalade and start away. As they drove off, he stepped back, struck the railroad flare and listened to it sizzle as he flipped it inside the cargo compartment where the bodies of his former associates lay in a heap. There was a rushing whoosh as the vapors exploded in flaming tendrils through the doors and windows just ahead of the tremendous burning. Black smoke rose, carrying the smell of burning flesh and upholstery into the now overcast sky as flickering red light danced in the foliage to the crackling of the disappearing evidence.

Jimmy picked up his cut from the heist and jogged toward the waiting car. He wasn't sure how much his share would cover but it should go a good way toward getting Irene the care she needed. If there was anything left over, he might see what Costa Rica was like. Let things cool off some. It hadn't been the easiest day's work but it would help settle up what he owed. Maybe, just for a little while, he could count himself a winner.

Since Robb's last appearance in the magazine has been gobbled up for inclusion in a prestigious anthology, I can only expect this one to be made into a blockbuster movie or something equally famous. One can't very well rest on one's laurels. Bigger, better, faster, or something like that. On the other hand, those guys are always looking for happy endings and crime fiction is, you know, crime fiction. Some of the best stuff rips your heart out...

Hansel Alone in the Deep Dark Woods
Robb T. White

His father was a crackpot survivalist, a doomsday prepper fanatic, who came home from his insurance job one day and announced they were leaving suburbia for a cabin in the Montana wilderness. He would never forget the stunned look on his mother's face or the blank expression on his older brother Tim's while they played Texas Hold'em at the kitchen table. Tim was about to turn over the river card just as his father came rushing into the house, waving his arms with the attaché case flying off the end of his fingertips; he looked at his brother with a blank expression, not saying a word. Tim simply got up and left the kitchen table where they often played a hand or two after dinner, sometimes betting on chores around the house or yard. The next morning Timmy was down at the Navy recruiting station and he hasn't seen him since.

When he turned seventeen, he stole the money his father had hidden in an empty Crisco can in the pantry and slipped out the back door. He made his way down to Iliad and hitched a ride in the back of a pickup with a friendly rancher who took him all the way to Great Falls. It was early spring and only the driver was dressed for the cold. Finally he rode a Greyhound bus south to Nevada and wound up renting a trailer in one of those parks where they preferred cash to checks and feral cats ran wild. It was thirty miles from

Las Vegas in a desert community of Mormons.

He remained there for eight weeks and rarely left except to go to the store. He was never sure whether he was more afraid his father would burst through the door in a rage at any moment. Sometimes he awoke before dawn thinking his father was staring at him from the end of his bed. It took some time for him to realize he was completely free and that he was never likely to see his parents or his brother again.

His old man had often ranted about Babylon, or America, "running out of time" when they went out hunting at dawn that used to fill him with dread. Now, free of his crazy old man, he felt Las Vegas beckoning with its promising glitter, urging him away from the cold and solitude of Montana. On clear nights, when the stars touched the horizon, he could make out the disc of orange smudge of the Vegas strip; it shimmered like a halo against the black ridge of the Spring Mountains.

He started small. He rolled middle-class drunks in parking lots. He looked for professional men who had wandered off the beaten path and wound up in some of the sleazier strip clubs. He learned quickly how to blend in and yet avoid contact with street people like the hookers and dopers, especially the meth freaks and the homeless, who were everywhere after some bars closed at three a.m. He watched cops brace them on the street corners, hustling them out of sight of the tourists.

He practiced with the sock and a bar of soap for weight on junk he picked up from roadside garbage. He was terrified of killing another human being but he accepted the fact his victims would probably have concussions to go with their hangovers when they recovered. He tore their wallets free from suit coats while they lay on the ground stunned; he searched pockets for loose bills men kept there to stuff into dancers' bras and garters. When he got efficient enough in his movements, he would remove a watch or ring if he felt the risk was justified. Besides being seen by a witness on these early morning prowls, he feared miscalculating the blow or, as had happened twice, missing the shot with a glancing blow and the victim turning and ready to fight. Fueled by alcohol, some drunks were dangerous. Most wouldn't report the crime because they were too embarrassed to explain their late-night outings to wives and girlfriends. At first when this happened, he ran away; then he grew confident enough to finish the job with a second swing. He kept his nerve until he sensed police cruisers were doing more patrols in the blocks he'd been prowling.

Two days later that changed; he would realize how lucky he was from the police beat section of the *Sun*. A UFC cage event was occurring that week and his last "victim," highly ranked in the welterweight division, reported the attack. What the paper had left out was the severe beating he had dished out on his would-be attacker. His assailant's left eye was swollen shut and two of his ribs had been cracked from the trained fighter's expert kicks. The cheek below his right eye socket remained a puffy bag of pus-colored swirls for a month afterward. He knew it was a miracle he didn't come to in a hospital bed. He lay on his couch moaning, occasionally jerking upright.

A week later, he changed job descriptions. As a teenager, he had never forgotten the thrill of leaping from high places, and so he began his second career as a second-story man. He traveled silently in the dark from one balcony to the next; he learned from the internet how to jimmy the locks on sliding-glass doors, and how to tell the difference between silver plating and real silver. While the occupants were asleep in their beds just a few feet away, he moved about in the darkness of their condos or apartments like one of those trailer-park cats. He was uncomfortable with his exposure to the fence he worked with, a woman pawn shop owner, because she could use him as a bargaining chip if law enforcement ever came around. Most of his money came from the objects he stole, very little from loose cash lying about.

He worked as a second-story cat burglar for two years, never taking big chances and always willing to go long stretches of time without a big payoff rather than push his luck. He upgraded his rental trailer with its ever-present odor of animal feces in the carpeting to a handsome double-wide in a better trailer park on the other side of town, where all the streets were named for desert flowers instead of presidents.

He kept almost all his "Armageddon" money, several thousand dollars, banded and divided by denomination, inside a chamois cloth he secreted in the duct work beneath the trailer along with jewelry and silver plate ware destined for his fence. In the afternoons, he watched boring shows or time-eating infomercials and studied real estate brochures. Abetted by Google maps on his laptop, these documents were a gold mine of information ripe with potential scores.

He preferred to operate in Sumerlin and Henderson, southeast of downtown Vegas. As tempting as the condos on the Strip might be, he knew they were too secure for a dilettante like him. He exercised fanatically every evening he wasn't out surveilling property. He focused on making his hands as strong as he could. He broke the springs in exercise grips and had to keep replacing them.

But even restricting himself to a disciplined low profile wasn't enough to keep the panic attacks from overwhelming him at odd times of the day or night. He could be sitting on his sofa watching TV or listening to the stereo or buying milk in a convenience store when they hit. He would find myself choking for breath as if he had just completed a marathon and be unable to control the hammering of his heart. He knew without a doubt his chosen livelihood was the root cause of the attacks, but that did nothing to make them stop. He ransacked a few bathroom cabinets for tranquilizers and opioids to try out at his trailer. They made him either leaden or nauseated.

The attacks grew more intense. Sometimes merely worrying about one coming on would often induce it. He had been forced to abandon his recon missions on his last three trips to Vegas. He drove home through the black desert landscape and sat in the dark until his thumping heart quieted of its own. On his fourth outing he headed for a certain apartment he had been considering for the past month. The owner, being a pit boss at a major casino, invoked fears of retaliation by the powerful casino establishment. They tended to take care of their own and they were efficient at pressuring police. He went over the details of the man's movements, which he always logged in his secret journal.

By the time he had hoisted himself over the balcony railing of the pit boss's condo on the third floor, he was shaking and his hands were trembling so hard he kept dropping the pick. Its tinny click was baffled by the high desert winds, but it sounded like thunderclaps in his ears. He couldn't go through with it and he was in no shape to attempt the climb down in the dark. Crouching behind a row of large potted plants containing Indian paintbrush, desert lilies, and scorpion weed that smelled like bad body odor, he waited for the first streaks of daylight to reach his side of the complex before risking the climb down. He knew he was all through as a cat burglar.

Before venturing far into his new career as a bank robber, he studied everything he could find online about bank operations, positions, and how they operated. His panic attacks had ceased, his "Armageddon" stash was at an all-time high, and he was finally able to ponder a few weeks of relaxation without the stress of work. He was tired of the road and the greasy diners. He was aware of the physical ailments long-haul truckers developed because of the starchy, MSG-poisonous diet they endured for years. Though he maintained his wiry strength with two hours of rigorous calisthenics in the motels, he often suffered from irritable bowels and his stool was frequently bloody. Of late, too, insomnia was fretting the good sleep he needed to perform at peak condition.

While washing the supper dishes that night, he broke a plate between his strong fingers and drew blood. Before he knew what he was doing, he was throwing the two pieces against the cupboard.

Without a further thought, he took a glass out of the drainer and threw it against the refrigerator. He upended the kitchen table with such violence that it shattered. In minutes, he had destroyed his entire kitchen—tossed knives against walls, smashed plates with Diego Rivera imprints, broke every fixture his powerful hands could find to twist or rip free. He collapsed against the sink with his arms hanging at his sides. Glass shards cut his flesh when he moved his arms across the floor but the pain felt weirdly good. He banged the back of his head against the sink ledge until warm blood flowed down his shirt. He ended sobbing on the floor for almost a half-hour; his tear ducts seemed to provide endless quantities of fluid. His head dropped to his chest and he remained in that position, unable to move or even flex a finger from the claws his hands had formed of their own volition. His overloaded brain had abandoned the citadel. His body in revolt had followed some crazy impulse of its own rather than rally around their host like soldiers defending their fallen leader.

The kitchen darkened by degrees but he was aware of nothing besides the sound of his beating heart. When the moon rose high enough to send a sliver of pale light across the floor between his outstretched legs, he thought of moving but decided against it. Three more hours passed before that thought occurred again.

"I need...to take...that vacation," he said.

He spent the rest of the day cleaning the mess of his kitchen and listening to Spanish guitar music "from the Balearic Islands" on YouTube. Halfway through the cleanup, his stomach heaved up a yellow bile; he realized he should eat something but the thought of food revolted him. He ate a trail mix concocted for his late-night expeditions. He lugged the shattered table outside and sensed his body was coming back to normal.

That night he went over his log and examined the time he had spent planning, surveilling, driving, committing the robbery, escaping, and covering his tracks. He made a calculation of his yearly takedown scores by matching the hours to weekly income minus living expenses. He was barely living a middle-class existence. He went online and studied certain professions and came to the depressing conclusion he was the equivalent, in every sense but the moral, of an entry-level claims adjuster for an insurance company—just like his father. In the bathroom mirror, he detected the same receding hairline at his temples performing its genetic jump from father to son. Just as it had from his grandfather to his father as evidenced in the black-and-white photos on the mantel back home in the time "before Montana." Even the fanatically detailed graphs and tables he drew up in his minuscule, downward-sloping script, produced an output that seemed to model that profession.

He had accomplished nothing by fleeing the cabin in the wilderness. He looked down at the writing and the diagrams on the last page—a branch of the Fifth Third in Seattle where it had rained nonstop for the two weeks he'd spent there. He shredded the notebook of his crimes in his powerful hands. He ripped all the posters of the Maldives off his bedroom walls, prints put up after his first score when he had deluded himself into thinking this was where he would wind up after his last job. He had spent hours staring at the turquoise waters and the magnificent sunsets and palm fronds waving by the shoreline. He vowed he would experience those warm sea breezes someday, and that thought alone caused his flesh to sprout in bumpy gooseflesh and raise the hairs of his arms; to smell that lemon-scented air and thrill to a parade of exotic girls in bikinis kicking up a froth of water as their long legs caressed the waters lapping at their ankles. A thousand times he had imagined himself watching them behind his sunglasses in a chaise longue while they laughed and moved down the shoreline as graceful as deer stepping through a meadow.

He threw the scraps into the air until the floor was covered in confetti. He slumped against the wall and folded himself into a tight ball with his knees tucked into his chest. He shook his heads from side to side and sprayed tears of rage at his self-delusion.

Sex was another thing. He hadn't had an erection in months. He'd always paid for sex with hookers in truck stops on monotonous interstates, which was all he had known of women and sex.

"I'm a joke!" he cried out to his empty living room. "It's all a fucking joke! All of it, all of it."

He became reclusive as a badger, rarely leaving the trailer. The cockiness of his early exploits was long gone. Now, it took little more than a hand moving sheers in the trailer across from him to spook him. For an entire month, he assumed he was under surveillance by federal agents. He lost weight and stopped exercising. Frequent migraines sent him into his bedroom where he lay for hours in the dark trying to bear the next five seconds of pain, then five more, and five after that, until he could sit up in bed without his gorge rising. Besides the crippling headaches and bouts of paranoia, he was becoming mentally confused about the simplest things. Once he tried to locate a spoon that was practically in front of his face yet he couldn't see it.

On one of his rare outings, he stopped by a Rite-Aid pharmacy for more migraine medicine, which delayed his return by twenty minutes and made him jittery. He was just about to make the turn into the park entrance when he noticed the lights on in the manager's trailer and a dark SUV parked out front. He spotted the discrepancy in license plates at once and he kept going straight. His stomach churned and he shivered, although he thought he had mentally prepared himself for this ever since he matriculated to bigger crime.

He drove to one of the many nondescript economy motels off the interstate. The lobby decor was heavy with Shoshone rugs, Paiute pottery and a bright Ute headdress tacked above a fake kiva in a small room where "guests could enjoy a free continental breakfast." He went to his room, undressed, and slept soundly, passing out as soon as his head touched the pillow.

Around midnight, he awoke with a foul taste in his mouth and his eyes gummed over. He dressed and took the stairs down to the parking lot. He made several passes along Bos Darc where his trailer park was situated but he detected nothing unusual. The manager's trailer office was unlit except for a light in the back at the opposite end where he conducted his business. His own trailer was visible from a parallel street; nothing unusual there either. No dark SUVs with federal license plates he could detect from a studied glance as he passed. He kept two lights on a timer switch when he left the trailer. Both gave partial views of the interior but he saw no one inside and nobody moving around. Everything looked completely normal.

He deemed it too risky to drive inside to see if his neighbors on either side were showing signs of unusual activity. If the FBI were lurking in shadows waiting for him, he was trapped. He returned to his motel room and slept until ten in the morning. He had a big decision to make.

After his shower, he sat on the bed with a towel around his waist and let his mind clear. He kept some money with a loaded Taurus in a go bag hidden in the spare tire well. It was a precaution adopted years ago. The rest of his stash, all the money squirreled away in the duct work might as well be radioactive because it could be years before it would be safe for him to fetch, that's if it were still there.

He dressed, left a tip for the maid, paid his bill in the lobby under the lens of the ever-present CCTV lens and headed for his car. He drove the speed limit all the way out of Nevada. Crossing the state line into Idaho, he felt as if life had given him a final chance. He wasn't prepared to spend the rest of his life in prison. He might even find a way to return someday to retrieve his money. Just past Saw-tooth National Forest he saw the sign for Twin Falls.

Keeping to his habit, he picked a motel off the highway. He found a family restaurant downtown and ate a leisurely meal with a slice of French cherry pie for dessert. He watched CNN back in his room for a couple hours and fell asleep. Around two in the morning, he heard noises from the other room; a bed was creaking and a woman's guttural voice called out in timed response to the throes of sex. He fell back asleep to the sounds as if he had fallen through a trap door.

The police officer who knocked on his door at seven in the morning was accompanied by the motel manager. Someone had broken into his vehicle while he slept; the windshield and passenger windows were fractured and the trunk had been pried open. His stomach lurched as they approached. The glove compartment was empty, the cover popped and hanging down like a broken jaw. His maps were scattered across the seat.

"Do you keep anything valuable in the trunk?" the officer asked him. He noticed the motel manager's brow was furrowed, concerned with his liability.

He took a quick look inside, his practiced face showing nothing. "Just the spare," he said.

"Looks like they moved it," the officer replied. "I'll need your driver's license and registration for my report."

"Certainly," he said and gave the cop a friendly smile. "I'll get it. It's in my wallet in the room. I won't be a minute."

Walking back at the same pace he used to follow drunks, he heard the manager grumbling to the cop. "Fuckin' dopers, always breakin' into cars around here."

His fake driver's license wouldn't stand a check and even if it did, the FBI might already have picked up a BOLO alert from the Nevada cops, and he couldn't take the chance.

He finished dressing in a hurry, fear worming its way into his esophagus. He headed for the bathroom window and saw at once it would be a tight squeeze. He used his folding knife to cut the bed sheet into strips and wrapped them tight around his chest. He clutched a bed pillow in his fist and punched the pebbled glass out. Some tiny shards were stuck in the aluminum frame. He hoisted himself to the ledge and with as much momentum as his hands could generate, he swung his body through the opening with the same grace of motion that once allowed him to traverse slender branches under his father's watchful eyes below. The cheap cement block construction of the motel would disguise any noise.

The drop was fifteen feet into a weed-shrouded ravine. A thicket of dock weed broke most of his fall, but his right ankle was sprained. He was hobbled by the pain, a red wave passed over his eyes with every step but he managed an ungainly trot in the opposite direction of the motel. He fixed his breathing to a steady intake. Tripped up by a gopher hole, he fell onto a tree stump; his arms came away with the bloody sheet in tatters where the embedded glass had ripped his sides. He still carried nerve damage there from that scuffle with the cage fighter. He hopped and stumbled for miles until he came to a stand of fir trees growing beside the highway. Cars drove past on the distant freeway, which meant he was too exposed. Instead of skirting the treeline he headed straight into it.

He found a trickle of water from a creek and a place to rest for the night as the light began to fade. Being this far north, he expected the air would turn much colder. Unless the moon showed a patch of light in its eastward orbit, he would remain lost overnight anyway.

There had been no sound of traffic for several hours.

He cleaned his bruised sides as best as he could with the torn wrappings from the sheets, but the icy water left him shivering against the trunk. Fear grew in the pit of his stomach as he reckoned the air was losing about ten degrees an hour. He foraged for dried leaves to bury himself in for the long night ahead.

"It's too late to change," he said in a halo of smoky vapor from his breath.

He thought talking to himself might warm himself up a bit. Night sounds were diminishing to a few shrieks from owls hunting vermin on the forest floor. "My father..." he started to say and stopped. An electric jolt of shivering made all his limbs shake at once, so he waited until it subsided and the twitching of his muscles let him speak aloud again. He knew from time spent in the cold winter mountains that the blood of arms and legs would abandon a person in the cold little by little for the security of the trunk. *To protect the heart.* He wasn't sure if he thought that or had said it aloud.

Time changed with the last light. The dark and cold of the woods put time into a different rhythm of its own devising It stretched like taffy one moment—then he remembered snapping to, as if he had barely crossed the threshold of sleep. He tried visiting the Maldives in his head. Soon the black in front of his face was palpable. He could not make out trees that were just feet from where he huddled with his back against the same tree.

His shivering eventually stopped but his hunger raged. His fingertips were so cold that they burned the sensitive skin of his ribs. His breathing came in quick panting breaths. He thought about getting up to stretch and tried to do so, but the mental effort was as exhausting as the physical. He tried to back trace his steps to the tree so that he could get out of the woods in the morning. His idiot father came to mind again. On one of their first dawn hunting expeditions, the old man tried to lecture him. He said that, if he were ever lost in the woods, he should compensate for being right-handed so he wouldn't circle back to where he started.

"Your right leg is stronger than your left," his father had said.

He smirked at that and his father became angry.

Why are you laughing, you damn fool?

I'm left-handed.

"I'm left-handed, Dad."

He realized he was talking to himself again. His father had missed every school event and all his Little League games, including his thirteen-strikeout shutout that made the papers.

"I've always been good with my hands," he said to the black trees. A wind had picked up and there was a gentle soughing above him. "My eyes, too. I've got 20/20 vision, both eyes."

His heart skipped a beat while waited for a response.

Nothing, nothing—

Then another panic attack hit. The fear, the racing heart, the confusion in his head.

"God damn it all, anyhow!" he cried and hunched over from the knife-sharp pain in his stomach as another wave of nausea rolled through. He leaned to the side to spit up the acid in his stomach.

"Fuck, shit, piss," he swore his favorite triad of words. But it was a hollow charm against the forces of darkness. Pinpricks of light tickled the corners of his vision. He started to hear sounds, different from the night-time forest sounds—weird howls and strange yelps.

"Oh fucking God," he muttered. "Wolves."

But it can't be wolves, he told himself. *That's—insane. I'm going crazy...*

The shakes started up again. His arms were now made of lead and he couldn't flap them for what little warmth that provided. The leaves he had gathered about himself were blown off.

The wind became a bone-chilling razor, twisting among the trees to find him, and cutting flesh wherever it touched.

Tears formed in his eye sockets and dribbled down his cheeks. After a huge, exhausting effort he made it to his feet with his back propped against the tree. His legs turned to rubber like some marathon runners approaching the finish line, and he found himself spraddle-legged on the ground like a baby chick.

He fell in and out of stupors that lasted for long minutes at a time. He remembered the Montana cabin and his mother's sad face in the doorway. He wondered if his brother was standing on the deck of a massive aircraft carrier somewhere in the South China Sea that very moment. He thought of praying but considered that as cowardly as confessing. Too late for God, too.

In a lucid moment, he found himself studying the tiny dents and ripples in the darkness. He was now able to make out the irregular shapes of some trees by their bark. Dawn was arriving. He was going to be okay. He breathed deeply to let the anxiety out of his chest. Then he saw his father standing in front of him.

"How did you find me?" he asked him. "What are you doing here?"

Anger overwhelmed him. "Go back to your cabin in the wilderness, idiot," he told his father. He tried to rise to confront the dark specter staring down at him from just a few feet away.

"You—you ruined—our family! For what?"

His father had no answer, but the *something* held its baleful stare.

He wanted to smash that staring face. "Don't you judge me, you fucker!"

In one final heroic effort to stand, he rose to his feet and took a step forward, fists clenched, poised to strike. He hit the ground in a deadfall that blew the fragile air out of his tortured lungs. His fists opened. He smelled earth close to his face, a musty, wormy smell of rot. He rolled over to look up at the trees where light was outlining branches in a muzzy pewter haze. His body was on fire. Bone-aching cold had finally vanished, replaced by a feverish, scalding heat flooding his arms and legs. The burning of nerve endings felt like the sting of fire ants chewing him from the inside out. His thick fingers tore at the buttons to rip his shirt free.

Get up, son. Let's bring your mother back a deer, hey?

C-coming, Dad.

While they walked, he told his father what he had done—all of it poured out in a single prolonged confession of shame and grief and sorrow from the time he had rolled drunks on the Vegas strip through his high-rise cat burglar phase to the bank stick-ups in a dozen states. His phantom father placed an arm around his shoulder as they walked through the bright woods together.

He wanted to tell his father something else—something urgent he had learned about being alone, something about hope, something crucial. But there was no more time.

In 2016 the Western Writers of America awarded Richard Prosch the Spur Award for his short story "The Scalper." His work has appeared in a number of anthologies and he's a lover of vinyl records, basset hounds and coffee. Richard's also an artist and an entrepreneur and in "Capitol Offense," he's very careful to not go overboard with a certain type of humor. Some of us have standards, after all.

Capitol Offense
Richard Prosch

Phase One of the capital city's renovation project meant the soft limestone of its central rotunda would be wrapped in hard steel scaffolding and blue plastic tarpaulins for the next nine months. A colony of orange-topped workers, like ants, crawling over every square inch of the century-old building. Sergeant Emma Floyd of the State Capitol Police didn't know much more than that. She got her news from the *Daily Gazette*, just like everybody else.

Standing inside a yellow tape barricade less than thirty feet from the machine deck of a massive diesel crane and sipping her morning coffee from a paper cup, she knew the project made her job on the statehouse grounds more complicated, but also—on days like today—more amusing.

Inside the crane's control cabin, a muscular guy wearing an orange hardhat ran the controls in a relaxed sort of way. The machine's engine roared, and a pillar of pungent black exhaust shot into the clouds.

Blinking against the sun, Emma watched the gantry glide away from the building. Steel cables threaded through an iron-trussed boom and stretching two hundred feet into the sky went into action, pulling up the main hook block and its septic burden.

The "King" Kelly Johns brand portable toilet, wrapped in fluorescent orange nylon restraints, rose above the maze of scaffolding.

"Time to clean the litter box," said Officer Tony Benjamin over the radio. Emma raised her cup in response. From his perch on the topmost landing, Tony waved.

Cleaning up after the fat cats. *It's what we do*, she thought with a smile. The sight of a lime green plastic outhouse, its reservoir filled—literally—with government waste, suspended majestically against the capitol's golden dome was pretty funny at that.

The sky was clear and the springtime air smelled fresh and alive. A row of ornamental pear trees in full blossom decorated the edge of the sidewalk.

"Let's keep the jokes to a minimum," said Emma into her shoulder mic.

"Good thing you're a sergeant and not a lieutenant," his voice full of good-natured humor. "I'd be calling you 'Loo.'"

"I just hope that toilet doesn't leak," said Emma, taking note of the King Kelly truck across the greenway on the street behind the tape, its flatbed full of empty replacement receptacles.

"Copy that," said Tony.

The boom inched to the north, swinging the portable lavatory away from Tony and the renovation site and out over the grassy promenade with its gardens of yellow tulips and gurgling granite fountains. Usually filled with school kids on field trips or an array of picnic blankets, that area had also been taped off.

A breeze picked up and Emma brushed away a lock of hair. On duty, she usually kept her long red hair pulled back in a smart bun, but today she went ahead and let it fall to her shoulders.

It was Friday, after all.

That's when the crane's engine belched and the King Kelly unit lurched sideways in its harness.

Emma's radio chirped. "Trouble, Sergeant," said Tony.

"On it," she said, stepping back from the crane to toss her cup into a campus trashcan.

There wasn't much she could do but watch as the boom jerked again, like an enormous fishing pole, dumping the load from its hook.

The green container answered the call of gravity, plunging straight down, crashing against grass and sidewalk with enough force to break its fiberglass shell and send a squirting geyser of blue-black liquid high into the air.

They'd been extra cautious in blocking off the area earlier that morning.

Thank goodness.

She keyed her shoulder mic. "What happened up there?" she said. "Did you see anything?"

"Not much. Looks like the harness snapped," said Tony. "Everything okay down there?"

Emma ducked under the tape and shot the shrugging crane operator a dirty look as she hustled past toward the wreckage.

"I think so," she said.

The King Kelly unit had hit right-side up but was split along its length and one wall had shattered into a half dozen pieces.

The lower holding tank was wide open.

The minty stench, overwhelming.

Coming up close to the broken side, Emma realized the surging puddle of waste was the least of her problems.

"Get down here, Tony," she said. "Get down here now."

So much for informal Friday.

Because there in the filthy rubble, the putrid form of State Senator Davis Hilton lay curled up in final repose, as though he'd found a cozy place for a quick nap.

Perfectly in character for Senator Hilton, only this time he'd never wake up.

It looked like Hilton had been pickling for several days. The stench of raw sewage was staggering.

Fighting back the natural reflex, Emma covered her nose and mouth, keeping her eyes wide open, taking in as much as she could.

There was no way the senator, or anybody else for that matter, could've been inside the toilet when the crane picked it up. Tony and the King Kelly rep had both been on the scene and would certainly have noticed the presence of a two-hundred-ten-pound man.

But here he was.

Senator Davis wore green pajamas, his trademark round spectacles, and a pair of red slippers. His arms and knees were tucked together, his hands curled up under his chin.

Emma walked the perimeter of the scene, stepping carefully, doing her best to record every detail.

And then Tony was there beside her.

"Holy cow, Sarge," he said. "Isn't that—?"

"Yeah. It is," she said, confirming the senator's identity. "Let's get this area secure."

"How'd it happen?"

"No idea."

Something in the grass caught her attention.

"Give me one of your gloves," she said.

Tony pulled off the yellow work glove while Emma took a pen from her breast pocket.

She picked up her discovery with the instrument and dropped it inside the makeshift container.

"What was that?"

"The senator's wedding ring."

After she talked to the crane operator, Emma met Tony beside the ME's wagon where it was parked under one of the pear trees. White blossom petals littered the sidewalk under her feet.

Tony was dressed in his black Capitol Police uniform, but wore an orange hardhat.

"You should be wearing a hat, Sarge," said Tony, patting the orange helmet.

"I'll take my chances," said Emma as her gaze swept the garden in front of the statehouse.

While she'd been questioning the crane driver, the press had arrived. Two local TV news vans had positioned themselves as near the yellow cement parking lot barricades as possible, and people carrying cameras and microphones were making their way across the grass.

Emma was about to key her shoulder mic when she saw Ed Jacobs, her station's communications officer running to intercept the reporters.

Sweet relief.

If anybody could hold back the gossip mongers, it was Ed.

"Crane guy didn't tell me anything I didn't already know," said Emma. "The engine sputtered a couple times, but the boom didn't jerk back hard enough that it should've snapped the harness holding the lavatory."

"So a faulty harness?" said Tony.

"Apparently. Though how the senator got inside the unit is a different story. I mean, you checked, right?"

"I'm telling you," said Tony, "there was nobody up there with me except the King Kelly guy who secured the harness to the crane. We both looked inside the unit. No way Senator Hilton was inside."

"You didn't rely on the little occupied sign on the handle and call it good? You actually opened the door?"

"Well, yeah. That's what I said."

"I'm just making sure."

"The john was vacant when it got picked up."

Emma looked across the grass at the vacant King Kelly truck. "Where's the company rep now?"

"I haven't seen him since I came down," said Tony.

"What's his name again?"

"Rick Ortiz," said Tony. "Nice guy."

"Okay. See what you can find out about him. Meanwhile, I'll go check on how the ME is doing with the deceased."

Emma watched Tony trot back toward the King Kelly truck.

If Emma knew the medical examiner as well as she thought she did, Jan Post would be finished and ready to roll sooner rather than later. The woman did not appreciate a crowd.

And the Capitol Grounds were promising a circus.

"You got a minute, Sergeant?" said a voice behind her.

Emma recognized Detective Paul Forest from the city police. She'd clashed with him before on cases where the lines blurred between her statehouse jurisdiction and the city's authority.

This time—with the death, accidental or otherwise, of a state legislator—they were both in position to get kicked out of the way by higher authorities.

"For you, I've got exactly one minute." She greeted him with a forced smile. "If you had a fresh cup of coffee for me, I'd give you two."

Forest was three inches taller than Emma, with dark hair he never bothered to comb and a day's growth of razor stubble. "So get me up to speed, missy" he said. "Davis Hilton is inside the potty when the crane picks him up and drops him a couple hundred feet onto the cement?"

"My officer says the senator wasn't in there when they started," said Emma. "And don't ever call me 'missy.'"

"Okay, okay. So, what—he was walking on the sidewalk and it landed on him?"

"No, he was definitely inside the thing when it landed."

"But you're telling me not when the crane picked it up?" said Forest.

"Apparently," said Emma.

"That doesn't make a hell of a lot of sense."

"It doesn't, does it?"

"Sarge?" A voice over the radio. "The ME is ready to get Hilton's body out of here."

"Take him through the carriage entrance to the lower landing," said Emma. "We'll meet you there," she said. "No cameras. The man's got a wife and three kids that don't need to see him hauled away on the nightly news with a puddle of crap in the background."

"Thing like this," said Forest. "A politician covered in excrement. The headlines write themselves."

"It's our job to get in front of them," said Emma, turning her back. "You coming?"

"Am I invited?"

"Hell no," said Emma. "But you'll tag along anyway."

Crossing the green, she made Forest hurry to keep up.

Jan Camp, the County Medical Examiner, was blonde with a high forehead that gleamed with perspiration on the coolest of days. Today, with the sun beating down, she looked like she'd just stepped out of the shower when Emma and Paul Forest met her on the lower landing of the Capitol Building.

Emma's phone chirped.

"One second," she said. A text from Tony.

She read the message and stowed the phone in her pocket.

Someone had brought the ME's car around and two paramedics were wheeling the senator's body into the back of an ambulance. Both of the vehicles were running and both were studded with flashing lights.

"What's it look like, Jan?"

"Looks like he's been dead a few days."

"So the crash didn't kill him?"

"No, he's been inside the tank for at least a day. Probably longer." Jan motioned toward the covered horizontal form. "Your typical porta-potty's a crock pot of chemical dyes, fragrance and biocides that feed on the waste. The senator's green PJs are actually yellow. He's been stewing quite a while."

Emma stared at the uncovered body, again taking in the mottled features, the bloated hands and puffy fingers.

"You're saying he was stuck inside the toilet's reservoir tank?"

said Forest.

"Yes, Detective. That's what I'm saying." Jan's scorn wasn't only reserved for crowds.

"How could he possibly have gotten in there?"

"Above my pay grade," said Jan. "That's *your* job," she told Emma, excluding Forest.

"Cause of death?" said Emma. "He didn't drown?" The thought made her fight a gag reflex for the twentieth time that morning.

"I don't think so. Can't be sure until I check the lungs, but he's got some pretty well-defined lumps and contusions."

"He'd take a few lumps just getting into the tank, wouldn't he?" said Emma.

Jan shook her head. "It's the damndest thing."

"The whole thing sounds improbable to me," said Forest. "Even with the lid up, the hole isn't big enough to force a person through."

"The whole thing is improbable," said Forest. "How does that tank come apart, anyway? He wouldn't fit through the flushing orifice."

"Maybe somebody took it apart. We'll have to ask the King Kelly rep about that—see if that's a possibility," said Emma.

"And where the hell is he?"

Emma thought about the text from Tony. "Missing," she said.

"Of course he is," said Forest. He turned to Jan. "You won't mind if I drop by the morgue later? I'll have a few questions for you."

Jan ignored him and walked toward her car.

"Good luck, Em," she said. "Keep me in the loop."

"You too."

"You guys got something going I don't know about?" said Forest.

"Get stuffed," said Emma.

"Apparently I wouldn't be the first guy today," said Forrest.

"Sarge?" Tony's voice over the radio. "I've got the King Kelly boss man here."

"Not the rep?"

"No. This is Mr. Johnson himself."

"Got it," said Emma. "I'll meet you."

As they walked back to the crash site, Forest's phone rang.

He dropped a few steps behind, staying within earshot. Then he called out, "Hey, Emma? What's the missing company rep's name?"

"Rick Ortiz," she said.

Forest repeated the name into his phone.

When he caught up with her, she added, "He's an undocumented worker. Probably took off at the first sign of trouble."

"You didn't tell me until now?"

"I just got the text while we were talking to Jan."

Then they were at the crash site.

"King" Kelly Johnson chewed grape-flavored gum like a first-grader and picked his nose. He was a red-faced, beefy man wearing a blue ball cap, black polo shirt and jeans.

"Sergeant Emma Floyd, Capitol Police," she said, shaking Johnson's callused hand.

"Pleased to meetcha," he said. "Wish it were under better circumstances." He reached into his shirt pocket, produced a glossy business card and handed it to her.

Emma glanced at it, taking in his home address.

"Hey, Paul," said Johnson, shaking hands with Detective Forest. "I was just telling your officer here how the King Kelly Mega-Throne goes together."

"You two know each other?" said Emma.

"Our kids play on the same soccer team," said Forest.

Emma nodded. Put her hands on her hips. "So, the, uh, *Mega-Throne?*"

"Your throne away from home," smiled Johnson.

Tony grinned. "There's a lever in the back, Sarge. It lets you open the bottom under the flushing orifice that allows us to change the holding tank."

"That's how the senator got in there?"

"Looks like it," he said.

"Still would be a hell of a lotta work to do it," said Johnson. He shook his head again, peering across the wreckage. "But that's probably how they done it."

"Who did?" said Tony. "That's the question."

Forest spoke up. "What about this Rick Ortiz, for one? You know how lawmakers are stirred up about illegals."

"Rick Ortiz ain't illegal," said Johnson.

A little too fast.

"His green card expired six months ago," said Emma.

"I've known Rick for three years," said Johnson. "He's a good man. A family man."

"Do you know where he is now?"

"I can't say that I do."

"You sent him down here this morning to supervise the removal of the Mega-Throne. Did Mr. Ortiz also oversee its installation on the scaffolding when it went up last week?" said Emma.

Johnson smacked his gum and appeared to be thinking.

"Yep," he said, finally. "Yep. We moved this unit up from my neighborhood."

"Your neighborhood?" said Emma, recalling the address on the card.

"Mine and Paul's."

"You're neighbors, too?" said Emma.

"We've got a playground under construction in our subdivision," Johnson explained. "Had the Mega-Throne in place along with three other units. But the construction got stalled. So when my contract had a scheduled potty-swap upstairs at the Capitol renovation, I had Rick bring this one over."

"Any idea why the harness failed?" said Emma.

"None at all," said Johnson.

Emma chewed her bottom lip, wondering at the workings of fate.

"If the harness hadn't let go—" she began.

"Ortiz would've gotten away with the senator's body," said Forest. "He could've disposed of it at his leisure."

"I don't buy it," said Johnson. "Like I said, Rick is a good guy."

"With a grudge against a politician who wanted to tear apart his family. It all adds up," said Forest. "I'll get a bulletin out on him."

"Except for the harness," said Emma. "Why would Ortiz rig it to fail if he didn't want us to find the body?"

Forest spread his fingers wide. "He didn't. The harness was just a fluke, Emma. An accident."

"And a lucky break for us," said Tony.

Emma caught herself staring at Forest's fingers.

Everything added up all right. Just not in the direction Forest wanted them all to go.

Or was that misdirection?

"Do you know what I love most about my job?" said Emma. "Tony, do you know?"

Surprised by the question, Tony shrugged. "Getting to work with me?"

Emma put her hand on his arm. "That's only in the top five," she said gently, giving him a wink as his cheeks turned red.

"No," she said. "The thing I like most is knowing that we hold a very special position here. We have a sacred duty. Not only to these grounds and the history they contain, but to the elected officials who work here during the session."

"I'm not following any of this," said Johnson.

"In a lot of ways, it's the best job in the world."

"Do you have a point?" said Forest.

Emma nodded. "My point is that one of the most important aspects of my job is to protect the legislators that convene under that dome. That means knowing them on sight. It means knowing something about their personal and professional lives. It means keeping up with their friends and family."

"And?" said Forest, scratching his ear.

"And knowing little details that aren't always public knowledge. Like knowing where they live," said Emma.

The three men waited for her to continue.

"Senator Hilton was your neighbor, wasn't he, Mr. Johnson? Your own home address is on the business card you handed me." She pulled the card from her pocket and handed it to Tony.

The young officer whistled.

"Prairie Heights," he said. "Pretty ritzy place. You could fit a basketball court in some of the living rooms out there."

"It's a nice area," Johnson agreed. "Scenic. Quiet. We've all put a lot of work and money into the neighborhood. Sure, Hilton lives out there. His property is right between Paul's and mine. The guy makes a mean pork barbeque." He pushed the cap back on his head. "Or, I mean, he did."

"Are you implicating Mr. Johnson in the senator's death, Emma?" said Forest.

"Nope," she said. "I'm implicating you, Paul."

"Me?" Paul's voice cracked like a teenager's. "What, are you kidding? Me?"

"You had access to the Mega-Throne. You had access to the senator."

"In his pajamas," said Tony, just as his phone buzzed.

"Makes sense to me," said Forest, his jaw clenched. "Why not blame me for the playground delay while you're at it. After all, I live right next door to that too."

Emma watched as Tony took in the message on his phone. Reading his expression, she smiled. He gave her a faint nod.

"Our guys picked up Ortiz," said Tony. "You'll never guess where he was."

Forest's jaw was moving faster than Johnson's now. And his face had gone pale.

"Tell us, Tony," said Emma.

"Trunk of Detective Forest's car," said Tony. "All taped up with a moon-sized lump on the back of his head. Says he was coldcocked. Making a heck of a racket now that he's awake."

Johnson stepped away from his neighbor. "Paul?"

Forest sneered at the three of them. "I won't stand for this," he said. "It's a set-up and you know it." He took two steps toward Emma and suddenly Tony was between them.

"It's okay, Officer," said Emma. "I think I've got this."

"You got nothing," said Forest, spitting on the sidewalk at her feet. "So what if I live next to Hilton? So what if I had access to the toilet? You still haven't explained that rigged harness."

"I'm betting Mr. Ortiz sabotaged the harness," said Emma.

"Which is what I said to begin with," said Forest.

"I think you told him to do it, Paul. Did you threaten him with deportation if he didn't go along with it?"

"In all fairness, Detective, you haven't explained how Mr. Ortiz ended up in your trunk, either," said Tony.

"This is bullshit," said Forest. "You two are trying to set me up."

"Ma'am," said Johnson. "If y'all would just slow down a second so's a guy could catch up. What I'm hearing you say is that Paul here is the one put Senator Hilton in the tank? But that would mean he's the one that killed him. Why would he do that?"

Emma shrugged. "Ask Paul," she said. "Hilton recently introduced a bill with some pretty stiff police regulation. Maybe that's part of it." She looked at Tony, but nodded at Forest. "Officer, please arrest this man."

Forest didn't resist as Tony cuffed his wrists behind his back.

"But you still haven't explained the harness," said Johnson. "You said Ortiz did that?"

"No matter who killed the senator, the thing I couldn't buy was the coincidence of the harness breaking," said Emma. "It's almost as if the killer wanted the lavatory tank opened up."

"For what reason?" said Johnson.

"Something incriminating?" said Tony.

"Maybe he dropped something," said Emma, reaching into her pants pocket.

She pulled out Tony's glove.

Again working with the pen she'd used to pick it out of the grass, she fished out something gold.

"When I first got to the scene, I was in a hurry," she said. "In my rush to secure things before anybody got here, I assumed this was the senator's wedding ring." She shook her head. "Later when we saw the body, I noticed his ring was right where it was supposed to be." She turned to Forest. "Unlike yours."

"I'm not saying another word," he said.

"Probably for the best," said Emma. She held up the ring to the morning sunlight. "Can you see the inscription inside the ring, Tony?"

He peered up and around the pen. "'To Paul,'" he read. "'All my love.'"

"Your mistake was only that you didn't get here soon enough," said Emma. "I found the ring before you even had a chance to look."

"Let's go," said Tony, marching Forest off the sidewalk in the direction the Capitol Police office.

The detective gave Emma a final, sullen glare.

"You know what they say, Paul," said Emma. "When you gotta go, you gotta go."

"I thought we weren't making any potty jokes today," said Tony.

"Just the one," said Emma.

"I think that was actually number two."

Emma crinkled her eyes and smiled at him. "Get him into a holding cell and get back out here," she said. "Just for that you owe me a hot dog."

And while she waited for Tony, she cleared her palette, bending over to smell the tulips, reaching for the ornamental tree blossoms, realizing with a shake of her loose red hair, that she really did have the best job in the world.

Lots of "Richards" in this issue for some reason. It just sort of happened that way. Or it's the next big thing. I guess we'll find out. This particular Richard is a photographer as well as an essayist on urban lifestyle and sustainable development, and of course a novelist and short story writer. His contribution here is close to but doesn't quite live up to its title.

The Last Word
Richard Risemberg

You'll never know who I am. And I don't know who you are. I wrote this out just the way I thought it, my dirty mouth and all, and it is what it is. Because I am what I am.

They say confession is good for the soul, so here's mine, nice and anonymous, because I'm nobody's fool. I've covered my tracks. I wrote this out in pencil, bought an old typewriter at a pawn shop— a typewriter, these days!—and I only touched the paper with wearing thin cotton gloves. Same thing with the envelope. Then I drove to another town to mail it to you, just a name, a random nobody I picked out of a phone directory online. I burned the pencil copy in the sink and washed the ashes down to the sea.

You should be intrigued, but if you're not, fuck you anyway. We'll never meet. You don't want to know me anyway. My hands are not clean. I killed a man—and not in war with the permission of some conclave of old fools, nothing but a paycheck and a kick in the balls afterwards. I killed a man because he was inconvenient to me. It had to be done. I'll tell you how it came about, if you'll bear with me.

The dead guy would say it was my fault—of course he would. And maybe he's right. You make up your own mind. I'm not going to take the blame for it publically. Nobility of mind is wonderful in other people—it's gotten me off the hook before—but it burdens the practitioner. I know; I've tried it a few times, strictly as an experiment, and it's cost me. I'm leaving it alone.

This is what you have to know: the man I killed was my brother. And not just my brother, my twin: identical flesh.

Not all twins get along, that's just another myth. Each of us is his own man with his own needs. The problem is that the other little fucker understands you perfectly. The opposite is true as well. You know what he's going to do to you, because you're going to do it to him if you get the chance. We were definitely not mythical twins. The truth is, each of us believed he should have been an only child.

We dedicated our lives to undermining each other at every possible opportunity. I'm sure that if I hadn't done him in, I'd be the one rotting away. I could say, if I was called on it, that it had been self-defense but that would be a lie. We were two bulls in one pasture; the hate was natural, visceral, vigorous. If Mom or Dad called me by the wrong name, I beat the other up as soon as I could catch him alone, and he always returned the favor. We tried wearing different clothes, different haircuts, whatever. Our parents worked hard and drank too much, and no matter what we did they still called us by the wrong names. Over the years the little scars we put on each other's faces should have been enough to set us apart, but the folks were so habituated to mixing us up that it didn't help. Even when we got older and started playing with beards and mustaches, it was fucking useless. We were too inconstant, that brother and I—new faces every month. I couldn't keep track of it myself: I'd look in the mirror and see him. One time I busted the mirror and added a new scar to my knuckle. That's the way it was.

From babyhood, we were rivals, never colleagues. Each keeping track of who got what and scoring love received by tally lists. And, listen, we were little stuffed shirts: once we learned how to read and write, we kept actual score in cheap pocket notebooks. Once we stole them from each other to see who'd come out ahead. Since our handwriting was the same, we ended up confused and didn't know who was best beloved, so in the end we had a fistfight and gave it up. After the tally sheet fight we were almost friends for a year or so.

But since then it's been Brits and Micks, Jews and Arabs, Hatfields and McCoys, whatever intractable drawn-out feud over nothing you can think of. Every once in a while one of us would make a peace offer, or some girl would play Kissinger to try to get us to make up, but she never knew the realpolitik of the situation…and then I'd pretend to be him, or he'd pretend to be me, and we'd take her to bed and act like a true lout and break up each other's good thing. It's no surprise neither of us ever stayed married. The women of the world don't know what a fucked-up life they're glad they're missing out on.

Well, a few of them got the picture. We got to be two old bachelors all too soon, stewing over bad memories and getting ready to make worse ones. Or we were, till I made the decision to kill the fucker. Half a century of crap was just too much for me. I wanted to die in peace, and that meant he had to go first and leave me the hell alone for a few good years. It was a drastic move but an easy decision. Remove the irritant, live in peace a little while, then die in bed. I thought of it as life-saving surgery. My life, of course.

I had to make sure I would really do it. I got to be honest: it's not so easy a decision to make when you're not really a criminal type. It must have been that love-hate relationship thing: we have to love each other to love ourselves, but we had to hate ourselves to hate each other. I lay in bed in the wee hours thinking back over the years, writing out the tally sheets in my mind, making them longer and longer. Not on real paper, no way: leave no evidence, in case someone got suspicious of whatever it was I was going to do. Remembering stupid stuff, like when I was coming in the back door of the house and the bastard threw a pan of chicken water at me, leftover slime from one of my mother's attempts at cooking. We were eleven years old. More serious stuff like answering the phone and pretending he was me when a girl I liked was calling, acting like the kind of asshole we both really were deep inside, and scotching my chance to get laid. This was when we were eighteen and getting laid was about the only thing on our minds. Really serious shit like running into my boss at a bar, buying him drinks, then pretending to be me and drunk and insulting the man and his wife, who was with him, and getting me canned.

He would gloat when he'd put one over on me. I was born ten minutes before him; to my mother this was a big deal, and maybe that started the whole thing. "Firstborn this, firstborn that," who gives a fuck? Well, she did. And we took it seriously. It was hate all day every day from then on. Tell you what, we should have teamed up like the twins of the cliché. But that's all sewage under the bridge; we were what we were, and he's dead and I'm not.

That's why you won't know our names. It's true what they say, criminals got to confess. So here it is, nice and anonymous, like I said, and fuck you too.

I planned the perfect crime, and it was truly perfect. Read on, you might want to try it sometime.

Years ago someone had taken me out on their sailboat, and I'd gotten the bug. I ended up buying a boat myself. Second worst decision I'd made in my life after being born. Of course that brother of mine had to buy one too, and his just had to be bigger and better. Not much bigger, not much better: basically the same model but four feet longer and ten years newer. My ex got the money from the sale of my boat when we split up—yeah, my brother jumped her pretending he was me, and she couldn't take that kind of shit—but the bastard had been smart enough, or mean enough, to get his own divorce before he got his boat, and he kept his.

When we were tolerating each other, we would sail it together. When we weren't, he could go drown for all I cared. Though I would've liked to have that boat. So anyway, I knew he still went out nearly every Sunday if the weather was right—because what else did he have to do? He didn't have any more friends than I did. Early in the morning he would motor out, set the sails when the breeze picked up, and head straight out into the ocean till he couldn't see the land. Just float around there for a while. It was the only time he and I could get along if I went with him. No talking except boat talk. The boat floating on the gray sea, the sky empty and blue, no sounds except the water slapping the hull, maybe a bird would pass by now and then to shit on the deck.

We would pretend to fish but really we were there because it was a place where you could peacefully not give a fuck about anything, even each other. A vacation from hating our lives. By the time we got back to the docks we would be growling at each other and usually get into an argument over something stupid. How to coil a rope, that level of stupid. But he was used to me just showing up. Maybe I was smarter than he was. Maybe I was just more of an asshole. What do you care? You're not my shrink. I decided I would kill the fucker on his own damned boat.

That was the easy part. Getting away with it might be harder.

At least I had luck on my side so far. I had a vacation planned, a trip across country to meet a woman I'd been corresponding with online. It looked good, and I didn't want that fucker around to ruin it. I was taking a midnight flight that Sunday, so I decided on an early boat ride in the morning. If things didn't work out exactly perfect, I'd have to give it up and let him live a while. That's just the way it had to be. You can't be impatient with a thing like this. You just can't be too patient either. Life is short even if no one murders you because you're an asshole.

I didn't need to set my clock. I always woke up before the sun, summer or winter. We both did. We were twins after all. Maybe if we hadn't been we could've left each other alone. No one will ever know. You don't get a choice of Life A or Life B. You just do what you have to do. I was wearing a beard then, and the asshole wasn't. I grabbed a razor and stuck it in my jacket pocket. If all went well—for me, that is—anyone on the docks when I came back alone would see the same bare face they were used to seeing when his boat came in. No one at home would see me without the beard, and I'd grow it back on the trip. I almost got stupid and called a taxi—habits will kill you sometimes—then I thought about ride logs and all that shit and took the bus.

I was plenty early. I made it to the marina before the sun was up. It was murky and gray, with a light fog. I was just another dipshit with a duffel bag walking toward the docks, another shadow in the dawn. No one was around, not even the fishermen. I heard a thump from the floating docks and saw my brother shuffling a styro cooler into the cabin.

I still had my key from the days of my own boat and I opened the gate, just like I belonged there. I don't think they'd changed the lock in fifty years. He noticed me as I walked down the ramp. Our usual greeting for a Sunday morning:

"Hello, asshole."

"Asshole."

He was ready for a nice, quiet time. And if things went well, he would get it. Forever, right?

Things went well. We motored out of the marina, him steering while I prepped the sails. As soon as we were out on the open sea, I hauled the sails up and he cut the engine. The wind was good, the way it always is at that time of the year, and we sailed along without talking, straight out from the coast to the usual spot. I remembered all the times we'd spent there together. The only good times we ever had. The boat moving the way it does on the water, no sound but the breeze. He spent most of his time out on the bows while I steered, feeling the wind, feeling the rise and fall of the boat on the low swells. The sun breaking through the mist now and then, everything smelling clean the way it never does in the city. Enjoy it, fucker, while you can. I didn't say it out loud, of course. I played our game. After three or four hours we came to our spot. Of course we didn't know exactly where we were, but it didn't matter. There was only empty water around us, no other boats, no planes in the air. The bastard had built his own coffin out of sea and sky.

He gave me the word to heave to—in boat talk that means set the sails a peculiar way one against the other so that the boat moves forward and backwards but doesn't really travel anymore, except to drift downwind. That was my signal to kill him too. He was bent over a locker digging up the fishing gear. I pretended to sneeze, then turned the boat the wrong way. He felt it and stood up to see what was happening—just in time for the wind to catch the big mainsail, the one that makes all the horsepower, and swing the boom around like a giant fucking baseball bat. Wham! It caught him right in the temple. He fell like a sack of gravel, out cold if he wasn't already dead. I set the boat right and got to work.

Every smart boat carries at least two anchors and most have three or four. But I found what I was looking for in the dinghy: a little rowboat anchor, home-made, concrete poured into a big coffee can with a ring bolt in it and ten feet of chain tied to a rope. I cut the rope with my pocket knife and wrapped the chain round my dead bastard brother. Clipped it good and tight round his middle, took his car keys and wallet, then had a quick look round to make sure we were still alone. Over he went, with hardly a splash.

And that's when he fucked with me one last time: as soon as he hit the water, his eyes opened, and he stared back at me with that look he has, looking me right in the eyes as he sank away. "Good-bye, asshole," I said. I even waved.

But then I didn't feel so good. My hands were shaking when I shaved my beard so that I'd look like him when we got back. I tried to check in the cabin mirror to see if I'd done a good job, and I had: it spooked me. I threw the razor into the gray water of the sea where it followed him down to the mud.

Still, I did everything perfect on the way back. Washed my beard out of the tin basin I had shaved over, even wiped the boom in case there was any hair on it where it hit him. Tied the boat up, waved at my neighbors on the dock, took my duffel to his car, drove it to his apartment, and left it there to take the bus to the airport. Everything nice and tidy. I could sit in the airport lounge for a few hours along with the rest of the lost souls and wait for my plane. Another sucker dreaming of a better place.

But even dead, the bastard kept fucking with me. The first time happened just a couple of days into my trip. The woman and I hit it off well—dinner and lunch out a few times, letting her show me the sights; in no time we were in bed. She wanted to cook for me the next night, and she was a good cook. Candles, you know, wine in the right glasses, leave the plates for later and get down to business. Like the dead asshole, I can be charming when it works for me. Breakfast in the morning, and like a good little gentleman who reads all the right magazine articles, I offer to wash the dishes, of which there's a double shitload. And that's when it happened for the first time: I couldn't fucking plunge the goddamn china into the soapy water.

Every time I tried I saw the fucker's face staring back at me through the suds, and the suds looking like the goddamn foam on the waves. This is the first time the woman hears me swear, and she comes trotting into the kitchen with those little worried steps they have, to ask what's wrong. What can I tell her? That my dead brother's in her sink staring me down with those sad fucking eyes of his? I just tell her I can't do it, I'm sorry. I can't even think of a good excuse, like I have a rash or something. I see the oh-oh look on her face, but then she smiles and says not to worry, she'll take care of it and we'll have us a nice day, won't we? All I can say is thanks and look like she just saved my life, which isn't going to impress her the right way. I can see that the mood of the trip is ruined, but I'm game to try to save the day.

Then when I go to the bathroom to brush my teeth I can't do it with my eyes open. Of course I see his face staring back at me. I know in my mind that I have the beginnings of my beard, but I just see him. I'm hoping she doesn't come in and find me brushing blind, but of course she does. I don't see her face because my eyes are closed but I can, you know, feel her stiffen up. That's two points against me right after our best night together. I hate the bastard more now that he's dead.

It keeps happening, everywhere. We walk around the city, and there's a park with a pond, and the water's not real clean so you can't see how shallow it is. There's big carp in it, and the game is to buy some fish food from a little gumball machine by the pond and feed the things, but I can't do it. I tried, but he's staring up at me from the thick green muck, just staring at me with that neutral what-the-fuck-I'm-dying-but-fuck-you look that he put on as he sank, and I can't even stand by the pond. The woman is looking at me like I'm a freak, which I guess I am, but it's worse because even the kids playing around the water are edging away from me, or their mothers are trotting up to drag them off. We walk on but I notice she's not staying too close to my side any more. And I've still got a handful of the goddamn fish food, which I throw at a squirrel, who at least enjoys it.

Lunch is a failure. The lump of sugar in my cup dissolves and his face floats up, and I fucking jump out of my skin. I can't drink the damn coffee. Now I'm starting to shake a little and swear under my breath. She doesn't know she's dating a murderer but she thinks I'm fucking crazy. And how can I explain without ruining everything? Then I start thinking dangerous thoughts: I've ruined everything anyway—or that bastard brother of mine has—so why not tell her what really happened? Then she'll understand why I'm acting this way. But I haven't gone stupid yet; I know that's a one-way ticket to the bughouse. I pull myself together. We keep walking but we're not talking anymore. I don't know what the fuck to do.

But she does. After a silent couple of hours seeing the sights she tells me it isn't working out. The asshole's dead and he's still fucked me up.

I spend the rest of the week drifting in and out of my hotel room and growing my beard back. It doesn't help much: I still see his face in the mirror when I brush my teeth. The only thing that does help is if I wear my dark glasses when I'm brushing my teeth. Fucking pitiful, isn't it?

The woman comes back once, thinking she was maybe a little too hasty, she spends the night, but in the morning she sees me brushing my teeth stark naked with shades on and she's out of there without a word. Just grabs her bag and shoes and runs out the door barefoot and looking pissed. I don't even go after her. The fucker beat me down again. I dress and go out into the hallway to grab a coffee from the machine by the elevators without even thinking about it, and the bastard's staring at me from the brown murk in the cup, those same sad eyes. I throw the cup down the hallway and run into my room. I look out the window at the city. That's safe, right? But I can't stand there forever. Eventually I got to take a shit, and when I turn to flush he's staring at me out of the fucking toilet bowl. He has no decency, floating up past the turds with those same sad eyes, fuck him!

What am I going to do? From then on I flush with my eyes closed. Holy shit, my life is a mess...

I go home. I should have had a message on my phone asking if I've seen the bastard, but it looks like nobody's missed him yet, or at least nobody's filed a report. He was a consultant, so maybe he was between gigs. And neither of us has many friends. That's good for me. But sooner or later his landlord or the dockmaster will notice that he's not paying rent. Someone's going to ask questions. I got to be able to keep my cool. But I can't even have a cup of coffee or a bowl of soup without he's staring back at me. He won't let up. He won't fucking let up.

And I can't let him get away with it.

That's why I sent this to you, whoever the fuck you are. He wants me to confess. That's got to be it. He wants me to tell someone and get picked up. That's the way it's always been, him getting me into trouble. The asshole's dead and he can't stop. You see what I've had to deal with? So I tell him, there it is, bastard: the confession. Someone's reading it. Someone knows. And even if they were God on a stick they couldn't find me, so fuck you, beloved brother. Feed the goddamn fishes.

I was going to finish with that and just keep it hidden in a closet, because I thought that maybe my writing this would be enough for him, but no: he showed up again and again. I went out my door just after the sprinklers had run and there was a puddle across the walkway, and he was in it, staring at me with his sad fucking eyes. I shrieked like a little girl and had to walk around it. My neighbor saw me. I went to take a leak in the middle of the night and I figure, it's dark, he won't be there. But the moon was shining in the window and there he was, staring up at me from the ripples of piss in the bowl. I jumped again and sprayed all over the place. I had to clean up, and then I was wide awake and couldn't sleep any more. He wouldn't let up. So I'm going to mail this to you after all, whoever you are. I'm giving my dead brother to you. What you do with him is your own fucking business.

I just worry that it won't be enough for him. When it came to bothering me, nothing was ever enough for him. We only ever got along on his goddamn boat. And I still have the key to the marina. If he doesn't let up after this, I have a plan to finish him off for good this time. He'd better watch out. I can find him again, I know it. He won't be able to resist sticking his mug up at me from where I dumped him. I'm going to finish this thing. I'll sail his own damn boat out there again and dive down and cut off his face, I swear it. The bastard...

He won't have the last word. No fucking way.

Next Issue

The very funny and very talented James O. Born is up with next issue's feature story. Jim is a veteran of just about every branch of law enforcement from Florida state to federal positions and when he's giving a talk at a conference (or his backyard barbeque where you should just feel free to drop in any time; no really, it's okay) he is not to be missed. His stories are fascinating and he's one of the most entertaining speakers you'll find. In the meantime, pick up one of his solo books or any of the number he's written with James Patterson or Lou Dobbs. So until next time...

Cheers,

BOOKS

On the following pages are a few
more great titles from the
Down & Out Books publishing family.

For a complete list of books and to
sign up for our newsletter,
go to DownAndOutBooks.com.

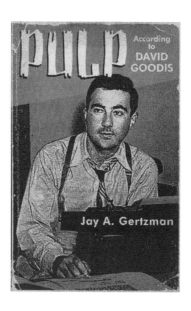

Pulp According to David Goodis
Jay A. Gertzman

Down & Out Books
October 2018
978-1-948235-36-5

David Goodis's novels mix realism, the disorienting, degeneration, and the dreamlike. Their narratives revolve around bottled up resentments, sexual fantasies (including incest), failure to combine trust with desire, and the trap of familial obligation. Goodis shows the way so-called escape literature with titles such as *The Moon in the Gutter* and *Street of No Return* can deal with personal suffering and hard-boiled nobility.

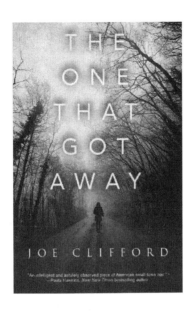

The One That Got Away
Joe Clifford

Down & Out Books
December 2018
978-1-948235-42-6

In the early 2000s, a string of abductions rocked the small upstate town of Reine, New York. Only one girl survived: Alex Salerno. The killer was sent away. Life returned to normal. No more girls would have to die.

Until another one did...

In Loco Parentis
Nigel Bird

All Due Respect, an imprint of
Down & Out Books
August 2018
978-1-948235-14-3

Joe Campion is the kind of teacher that any child would want for their class. He's also the kind of teacher that lots of mothers want to have. And some of them do. When he becomes aware of the neglect and abuse suffered by a pupil in his care and witnesses an explosion of rage from the music teacher in the school, he decides the systems to deal with such instances aren't fit for purpose. It's time for him to take matters into his own hands. His impulsive nature, dedication to his pupils and his love of women lead him into a chain of events that would cause even the most consummate professional to unravel.

The Carrier
Preston Lang

Shotgun Honey, an imprint of
Down & Out Books
July 2018
978-1-948235-02-0

It's a bad idea for a drug courier to pick up a woman in a roadside bar. Cyril learns this lesson when the sultry-voiced girl he brings back to his motel room holds him up at gunpoint.

But he hasn't made his pickup yet, and the two form an uneasy alliance in a dangerous game to grab the loot.